# CHASING TROUBLE

## Trouble In Love Series

## SONIA STANIZZO

Chasing Trouble



First Published by: Beachwalk Press, Inc. 2018

Second Edition: 2021

ISBN: 978-0-6450908-5-7

Publisher: JRL Publishing

Editor: Lynne Sully

Cover: Outlined with Love Designs

*To Mum. Thank you for passing on your love of reading. I miss you every day.*

Chapter 1



Nick Williams sat alone in a booth at Dexter's Pub, a glaring gaze fixed on a woman he'd hoped never to see again. Ava had left town ten years ago, and seeing her again was like a knife twisting in his gut. Over time he'd learned to push the memories of the few months they'd spent together into the deepest part of his mind, but now they came rushing to the surface. Her leaving being the clearest one.

She sat sipping on a cocktail at the bar, unaware of his presence. Her tongue darted out and licked something off her bottom lip. Once the small gesture would have sent a firestorm raging through his veins. Now a cold emptiness settled in instead.

Feeling disappointed that she still provoked a reaction from him, he turned his head and stared out the nearest window. Farmers and tradesmen were finishing work for the day, and the carpark was quickly filling with work utes and beat-up cars. Black clouds cloaked the setting sun, pitching the mountain landscape into darkness.

He'd come to the pub outside of Sunland Valley, hoping to relax and enjoy a cool beer after working long hours at the workshop. It had been ages since he'd worked with tools, and he had to admit he'd missed it. Nick turned his palms face up. A satisfied grin tugged at his lips as he gazed at his grease-stained, blistered fingers. Spending the past six years behind a desk had made his hands soft. Now they no longer belonged to the pen-pusher he'd become.

"Boss, you're gonna burn a hole in the back of her head if you keep glaring," Ben said as he slid in the booth opposite him and twisted the lid off his Corona.

Nick's fingers clenched around his own cold bottle.

Ben leaned his elbows on the table and nodded toward the bar. "You gonna ignore Ava's in the room or are you gonna go and say hi?"

Nick pinned him with what he hoped looked like a fuck-you glare.

Ben shook his head with mock pity. "Boss, boss, boss."

He'd started calling Nick *boss* the day Nick had given him a job at the workshop as the head mechanic. It began as a joke because he knew Nick hated it, but over the years it had stuck.

"Are you scared to say hi?"

"I'd rather pull my teeth out," Nick muttered.

Ben slapped the table and laughed. "It can't be that terrible seeing her again."

Nick glanced toward Ava, hoping Ben hadn't attracted her attention. Thankfully, she was busy looking into a small mirror and reapplying lipstick. It was worse than terrible, because he thought if he ever saw her again he'd feel nothing. No hurt, no anger—nothing. But bad blood still flowed in his veins.

"Boss, what's it been, seven or eight years since she left? Surely you're over her leaving, and you'd have a shit-load to catch up on. Does she even know you're as rich as freaking Bill Gates? You're not the poor, little mechanic her father warned her about."

Nick's laughter had an edge that didn't sound amusing. "I'm hardly Bill Gates, and to Ava I'm still the poor, little mechanic her father warned her about, and that's how it will stay. She doesn't need to know what's in my bank account." He took a long swallow of his beer and banged it back on the table. "In fact, she doesn't need to know anything about me, because I have no intention of *catching up*."

With a raised eyebrow, Ben lifted his palms up as if to ward off Nick's bitterness and pushed himself up from the booth. "No problem, boss. My lips are sealed. You're not in the greatest of moods tonight, so I'm gonna see if Jane's home." He winked suggestively.

"Hopefully, she'll be more entertaining."

When he left, Nick's attention was drawn back to Ava. You couldn't help but notice her. It was like a queen sitting amongst a group of commoners. Her smooth, olive skin had not been affected by age, and the fitted white pants and clingy pink top hugged her in the best possible way. Black, glossy hair fell just below her chin, shorter than she used to wear it, framing her oval face. Grudgingly, he could admit she looked damn good, but he'd bet his Porsche Spyder that her heart was still cold and vindictive.

A beefy guy with jeans so tight Nick wondered how his nuts weren't in his throat, sauntered over to Ava and sat on the stool next to her. Turning to him, she beamed him with a killer smile. After a moment, the guy slid his hand onto her hip, and she removed it with a quick flick and a playful slap on his arm. She said something with a laugh. The beefy guy ducked his head like he'd been chastised, but he didn't hide the glimmer of his intentions.

*Good luck to the sucker.*

There'd been a time he'd wanted her too. And wanted more than just her body. He wanted a life with her. But she'd jumped into her BMW and left without a backward glance. *Left him.*

He rubbed a hand over his face. God, he needed to scrub these thoughts from his mind. It was time to get the hell out of Dexter's before getting spotted.

But before he had the chance to move, she stiffened in her seat and scanned the pub. When her gaze landed on him, her eyes widened, and the dazzling smile she wore for the beefy guy dropped.

Nick held his breath.

*Busted.*

Ava Cardona tapped her foot at a rapid pace on the stool at the scarred, timber bar, sticky from spilled alcohol. With a straight back, she sat sipping her favorite drink, a margarita. The bartender had given the order a funny look. She supposed it wouldn't be a common drink in Sunland Valley. The pub was filled with farmers. Their go-to drink would consist of a cold beer or a shot of whiskey.

She'd stopped at the pub outside of town because she wanted to put off going home. Her stomach dropped and her chest tightened. She hadn't called Sunland Valley home in years. She'd moved on, found a new place to fit in, and left the scars of her past behind.

A call from her younger sister had brought her back. Isabella needed help with something that couldn't be done over the phone. She'd said it *must* be face-to-face. Probably just some teenage drama. But what if it wasn't? Bella had never asked her to come home. It really could be important.

Guilt sat heavy on Ava's shoulders for not spending more time with her sister. Anything Bella needed or wanted was done over the phone. Or while on school holidays when she'd stay with Ava on short visits. But it wasn't enough time.

Ava had her reasons for staying away from Sunland Valley, and their father was one of them. Her relationship with him died the day her mother killed herself in a car accident. And she never thought she'd ever come to terms with his involvement.

But she loved Bella very much, so if she had to face her father to help her, she would.

"Hey, honey, mind if I join you?"

She flinched and swung around to look at the heavy hand on her shoulder. The man belonging to that hand didn't wait for a reply and sat his over six-foot, solid frame on the empty stool next to her.

Two dimples dented his tanned, weathered cheeks as he smiled and pointed to her drink. "That looks too posh for me. Tommy, I'll have a Pure Blonde," he called to the bartender then winked at Ava with a mischievous gleam. "And a black-haired beauty if she'll have me."

She nibbled her bottom lip and let her gaze travel over the cute guy with the dimpled cheeks and great body. Maybe he was the distraction she needed. Anything to keep her mind off going home.

"I know I've never seen you here before." A confident hand slid onto her hip. Instead of her body tingling in a good way, her stomach tightened and her skin itched. She wanted his hand off immediately. It wasn't the reaction she'd hoped.

Hiding her discomfort behind a playful laugh, she flicked the offending hand away.

"Now wait a second, sweet-cheeks, you haven't even bought me a drink."

He ducked his head then called out for another of whatever she was having.

Normally Ava enjoyed a good time with an attractive man, but this country boy with a cocky smile was too sure of himself. And her interest in him, no matter how good-looking he was, was low. In fact, her interest in men, which she liked a lot, was minimal lately. Maybe if she gave him a chance things might change.

Then he used the cheesiest pickup line ever, and she'd heard her fair share. "Your lips look so lonely, baby. Would they like to meet mine?"

Dammit, the microscopic interest level plummeted to non-existent. The country boy would have to try his pickup lines on someone else.

Before Ava could say he was wasting his time, a niggling sensation like a thousand tiny, icy spider legs crawled up her spine. She stiffened in her seat. The uneasy vibes weren't coming from the country boy. His dopey smile was harmless enough, even though he did have roaming hands. So she scanned the dim room, and her gaze stopped cold when she located the cause of her unease.

*Nick.*

Body tensing, her heartrate kicking up to a dangerous speed, she stared at the hard face watching her. The man who had once torn out her heart sat in a dark corner of the room. A navyblue trucker's hat pulled low over his face, midnight hair flicked out from under it. A gray t-shirt pulled across broad shoulders.

As their gazes collided, he straightened his shoulders and lifted the cap. When noticing her scrutiny, he slid an arm over the top of the padded booth and a slow smile as dangerous as the devil's twisted his lips. But she wasn't fooled by his laid-back demeanor; he held his beer bottle white-knuckle tight.

Ava's bar companion leaned closer, and she cringed at

his stale beer breath. "How about coming to my place? It's not far."

At the sight of her old boyfriend, a strong buzzing sound vibrated through her head. Without taking her eyes off Nick, she replied, "Sure, just give me a minute." She didn't even know what she'd agreed to as she slid off the chair.

With muscles quivering, Ava weaved her way between the tables until she reached Nick. She slapped her palms on the tops of the sticky table, leaned toward him, and whispered on a low growl, "What the hell are you doing here?"

Nick had asked himself the same question. As soon as he'd seen Ava sipping cocktails and chatting up the beefy guy, he should have run for the hills. But before he got the chance, she'd pinned him with those toffee-colored eyes filled with loathing.

Swallowing the rest of the beer, he wiped his mouth with the back of his hand, and trailed an insolent gaze over her. Hoping she'd understand he wasn't happy for the reunion either.

"No hello? Oh wait, I forgot. You like to skip the hellos and *goodbyes*."

Anger burst bright from her eyes. What the hell was she angry about? She was the one who left without a word.

"I thought you'd be long gone from Sunland Valley by now," she spat.

"Looks like the town needed a good brothel after all." At the mention of the brothel, for a second, he thought he'd seen a flash of guilt pass over her face, but then it disappeared in a blink. "The men in this town are thanking me, but their wives…not so much." He gave her a two thumbs-up gesture. "Thanks for the great business opportunity."

He'd never let her know she'd almost ruined his chances of building a successful career with the outrageous rumor she'd started before leaving town.

A smug sneer twisted her lips. "Are you still living in Sunland Valley? What happened to your big plans to leave and conquer the world?"

Leaning back in the seat, he spread his arms out wide. "Who needs to conquer the world when I'm here living the dream."

"Nobody wanted you here." A neat eyebrow rose.

He gritted his teeth. "You made sure of that, didn't you?"

Once he believed she could see past her father's money and love him for who he once was. He'd been wrong. She was quick to run with a better offer.

Before Ava could respond, Nick flicked a glance at the beefy guy she had been drinking with, who was now making his way over to them. "Your date's getting lonely."

"What?" Confusion lined her face, and she glanced over her shoulder just as beefy guy slid his hand on her hip, pulling her close.

She stiffened but beamed him with a smile bright enough to light up a small city. The guy was practically drooling.

"How about we take off, babe?" he asked.

"Yes, let's go." Placing a hand on the guy's chest, she slid Nick a look. "Wish I could say it was great seeing you again."

"Yeah, I wouldn't put this in my top ten favorite moments either."

## Chapter 2

Nick wanted to order another beer, listen to crap country music, and forget about seeing Ava. But no amount of alcohol could erase the unpleasantness of their reunion. God, hate still festered like an angry ulcer in his gut.

Slapping a fifty-dollar note on the table, he waved goodbye to Tommy, who was wiping empty tables. He couldn't sit there any longer or he'd be walking down memory lane with Ava in the spotlight.

Outside, clouds hung low and enveloped the night sky, and a strong wind blew through nearby trees. The forecast promised a storm, and Nick could smell the damp air as he walked to his truck.

A noise to his left caught his attention. When he turned, Ava and the beefy guy were leaning against a silver Mercedes. The beefy guy's face was buried in her neck, and his hands were on her arse. Nick shook his head. They couldn't even wait until they got inside the car.

He unlocked the door, slid onto the cracked leather seat of his Toyota Hilux ute, and watched Ava. The hook-up must not be going too well because she shoved the guy away, removing his roaming hands from her body. But apparently the guy was too thick to get the message, because he continued to pin her against the car, ignoring her protests.

Nick's fingers gripped the steering wheel. The last thing he wanted was another confrontation with Ava. But he couldn't sit around and watch a man roughen up a woman, even if that woman was Satan. Sighing, he tilted his head back on the headrest for a beat then dragged himself out of the truck. Just as he reached Ava, the guy screamed in falsetto and dropped to his knees, clutching his crotch.

"You were always a ball buster," Nick said as he dug his hands into the pockets of his jeans. He cocked his head toward the man moaning on the ground. "Though I reckon he deserved it."

Ava ran her hands through her hair and all the strands fell back into place—back to looking immaculate, like she didn't only moments ago take down an overly-muscled son of a bitch.

"What the hell are you doing here?" Ava asked him for the second time. He knew she didn't mean in the carpark, but he had no intention of sating her curiosity.

"Trying to help."

She slapped her hands on her hips and narrowed her eyes. The sharp look she threw him said she knew he was avoiding answering the question. "I had things under control. I didn't need your help."

They paused their standoff to watch the beefy guy struggle to his feet, still clutching his balls. Nick heard him mumble something about "fucking crazy bitches" as he staggered back to the pub. Nick agreed one-hundred percent.

"I'm sorry I tried to help. It won't happen again." With that, Nick left without a backward glance.

Once he was seated in his truck, a Mercedes, with Ava in the driver's seat, sped by him and out of the carpark. He didn't know why she was back in town but hoped whatever her reason, their paths didn't cross again.

Big, fat raindrops splashed onto the windscreen, and he flicked on the wipers. These days he rarely thought about her. He'd forced her memory down in the deepest part of his mind. But every time he came back to Sunland Valley, memories of the time they'd spent together, running wild, cracked through the barriers and wormed their way out.

As he drove toward home, the rain grew heavier and smashed hard against the roof of the truck. The frantic swipes of the wipers didn't do much to clear the water from the windscreen. Small rivers filled the gutters, and Nick wanted to be home before he got caught in flash flooding, which this area was prone to have.

He traveled along Woodland Road when up ahead, flashing yellow hazard lights on a silver Mercedes illuminated the stormy sky. The bonnet of the car was propped up, and Ava leaned over it while trying to grip onto a black and white spotted umbrella.

"She doesn't need my help." Didn't she tell him so a short while ago? He slowly drove past her.

An expression of hope that someone might stop twisted into a scowl when he kept going. Obviously, she didn't know who was in the driver's seat, because he had no doubt she'd want him to keep driving.

Yeah, he was being an arsehole. But surely someone would drive by and offer her a hand.

Then he glanced back in his review mirror just in time to see Ava's umbrella flick inside out. She threw it on the ground, and the wind picked it up and it went tumbling into a cow paddock. She held up a mobile phone high above her head, looking for a signal. *Good luck finding one.* They were in a ditch with dodgy reception on a good day. It would be impossible to get one in this weather.

He blew out a breath. As much as he hated to admit it, he couldn't leave her out there in the dark, especially with the full force of the storm about to hit. His mother had raised him to be a decent human.

"Dammit!" Nick pulled to a stop, smacked his palm on the steering wheel two times, and growled a sigh.

He did a U-turn, drove back, and pulled up in front of her car, pinning her with the headlights of the truck. She held her hand up to shield her eyes from the bright lights. When she must have recognized him, she frowned, swung her back to him, and poked around in the engine with her index finger. Yeah, like that would solve the problem.

Nick ripped the cap off his head, tossed it on the cracked dashboard, and ran his fingers through his hair. Of all the women in the world to be broken down in the middle of nowhere, why did it have to be Ava? Why not Tania from the feed supply store? She'd been getting friendly with him lately. Christ, he'd even rather it be old lady Eliza who owned the adjoining farm. She believed Nick was the reincarnation of her late husband and often mentioned what she'd like to do with him inside the hay shed. And it wasn't counting inventory. Damn, she was nimble for an eighty-eight-year-old woman. He'd gotten his backside pinched a time or two.

Nick wound down the window a crack. "Having car troubles?" he yelled through the gap.

Ava stiffened, glanced over her shoulder, and yelled back, "Nothing I can't handle."

"Bloody stubborn woman. I should leave her out here."

Nick peered through the thrashing wipers. The thought of getting wet was unappealing, but the sooner he got Ava on her way, the sooner he could get himself home to a warm, dry house. He pulled out a waterproof jacket stuffed behind the headrest, put it on, and shoved his cap back on.

When he opened the door, the force of the wind sprayed rain as sharp as needles into his face. *Fuck!* How was she standing out here wearing practically nothing? The white denim jacket she'd added to her skimpy outfit wouldn't be doing her any favors. The clothes plastered her body, and he took a moment to allow his gaze to roam. Just because he couldn't stand Ava didn't mean he couldn't appreciate her drop-dead gorgeous body.

"You know, I've never seen a car repaired by poking."

Ava whirled around and threw daggers with her gaze. Turning back to the engine, she then used two more fingers, and this time rattled some hoses.

Nick shook his head.

Opening the Mercedes's door, he slid onto the soft leather seats. She stomped over to him before he could close the door.

"What the hell are you doing in my car? You'll ruin the leather with your wet arse." She pushed a lank, wet strand of hair away from her face, streaking a smudge of grease across her cheek. "You'll pay to have it re-upholstered. Oh my God! Water is all over the controls on the door!" She shrieked so loud he thought he heard the cows in the paddock trot away.

"If you keep standing there blocking me from closing it, it will only get wetter."

She quickly stepped back and slammed the door. There was no mistaking the word *bastard* on her lips. Why was he helping her again?

He flicked the ignition a couple of times, and it made a cranking sound. It didn't sound like a flat battery. Dammit, why couldn't it be as simple as the battery? Then he would've been able to jump-start it and watch her drive away. There was no way he could fix the car on the side of the road. It needed to go to the workshop.

He flicked out his wrist to check the time. There was no point calling Ben for a tow truck. He'd be with Jane, and it would have to be an emergency for him to leave. Nick was tempted to tell him it was a life-or-death situation but knew he'd never hear the end of it if he called him out in this weather.

He got out of her car and threw her the keys. A hand shot out to catch them.

"Well?" she said and crossed her arms over her chest, shivering as the rain pelted them.

"What's wrong with my car?"

Her folded arms caused her breasts to lift and the jacket to open. His gaze dropped to the raised peaks of her nipples, and he inwardly groaned. He pinched the bridge of his nose and trudged through the mud to his truck and away from the *headlight* show. "I think it's either the fuel pump or an electrical problem."

Her voice rose. "You're going to fix it, right?"

"I can't on the side of the road."

"You're not going to just leave it here?"

"Yep, there's no one who can tow it tonight." He opened the truck door and paused; the words about to be spoken tasted like ash on his tongue. "Want a lift?"

Her mouth opened and closed a couple of times before she shut it in a firm line.

"Get in…or don't. I really don't care. I'm getting in, my balls have just about disappeared."

For a second her gaze flicked down to his crotch, and when she spotted his knowing grin, she straightened her shoulders, stuck her nose up in the air, and didn't budge.

"Suit yourself. Good luck getting a ride tonight." He jumped in his ute, turned the ignition, and cranked on the heater. Unzipping his jacket, he shrugged it off then threw it behind him. Spring had provided beautiful, warm days, but the nights still had a chill. The water that had soaked through his clothes only made it colder.

A crack of lightning lit up the sky, and Ava scrambled into his truck just as the thunder boomed and rattled the windows. Nick didn't bother hiding his smirk. She was still scared of thunderstorms. He pulled back onto the road and navigated his way through the dark, stormy night.

After a moment, she said through gritted teeth, "I guess you're going to gloat."

Nick didn't take his eyes off the road when he replied, "No."

She tilted her head to the side and squeezed water from her hair. "I don't believe you. I bet you're dying to rub it in my face that I needed help and *you* came to my rescue."

"I would've stopped for an injured animal. Don't think you're anything special."

She huffed.

Nick knew he was being an arsehole but didn't care.

Another lightning strike illuminated the sky, and she covered her ears, preparing for the thunder soon to follow. When it did, she sprung so high she almost bumped her head on the roof of the truck.

"Still scared of a little storm? We're not going parking like we used to, so I can't distract you."

She whipped her head around and stared wide-eyed at him.

Crap, why did he have to say that? Nick didn't want to think about what they got up to in the past. Shifting in his seat, he scrubbed a hand over his face. To change the subject, and because her shivering vibrated against the seat, he said, "There should be a jumper behind you." She twisted around to reach behind the seat, and her breast brushed up against his arm. His already firm grip on the steering wheel tightened even more, and he ignored the rush of heat heading south.

"Where am I taking you?" His voice was hard.

She raised an eyebrow at the harsh tone. He wouldn't pretend he was happy about being in such close proximity, especially with how his body was reacting.

"I have a room booked at a bed-and-breakfast. It's called Greenhill House. It wasn't around when I lived here. Do you know where it is?"

"Yes." He owned the place. He didn't question why she wasn't staying with her father.

The less he knew the better.

"Of course you would since you still live here."

*So Miss Universe thinks she's the only one who got out and spread their wings.*

"Just don't ask me to take you anywhere out of town, because I might get lost." Sarcasm dripped from Nick's voice like the rain on the windshield.

She didn't apologize for the insult, not that he really thought she would. Instead, she glanced around the cabin of the truck and laughed with disbelief. "Is this the same truck you drove years ago?"

Tempted to drop her off on the side of the road, Nick drew in a deep breath before answering, "Yes."

She ran a hand over the cracked vinyl seat. "It's not very comfortable."

"You never complained. You used to beg me to take you parking in it so we could fu—"

"I did not!" she interrupted.

He couldn't believe he'd brought up their time together again and wanted to drop it fast. "Sorry it's not as luxurious as your Merc." Leaning forward, he squinted through the rain and pulled to a stop. "Shit…"

Ava followed his gaze. "What?"

"The road into town is flooded. We can't cross."

"Are you telling me this town still hasn't fixed the problem with this road flooding?"

"I'll have to bring it up at the next council meeting. Just for you."

"Isn't this a four-wheel drive?" she asked, ignoring his sarcasm.

"Yes."

"Then what's the problem?"

He gave a heavy sigh. "It's too deep. We could get washed away."

"We can go back and get into town from the highway."

Did she think he was a freaking Uber? "It will take an hour just to get back to the highway and then another forty-five minutes into town. I'm not driving unnecessarily in this weather."

Nick slammed his fist against the steering wheel. All

he wanted to do was go home after a long day, put his feet up, and watch sports. The Flaming Stars were playing in the semi-finals tonight. How did his day turn to shit?

Slumping in her seat, Ava asked, "What do we do now?"

"You have two choices. I take you back to your car and hope it's comfortable for you to sleep in or..." The next words clogged in his throat.

Ava sounded reluctant to ask, "Or what?"

He cleared the lump. "You stay the night at my place."

------

Chapter 3

------

The pounding rain and the whooshing sound of the windscreen wipers filled the awkward silence in Nick's truck. A blanket of darkness cocooned them within the small space. The thunder and lightning display was tame compared to the irritation radiating from Nick.

Nick was the last person Ava wanted to see when she'd arrived back in town. Sunland Valley held too many hard memories, and Nick ranked first. And why did he have to go and remind her of the last time they were in a storm in this truck?

Even though it was a long time ago, she remembered they had passed the time doing such a great job fogging up windows that she didn't notice the wild weather. Things were wilder in the truck. She shook her head to release the image. She couldn't help being stuck with him on a dark, stormy road, but she'd rather gnaw her own arm off than request more help.

In the hopes he was wrong about the flooded road, she asked, "Are you sure the water's too deep to cross?" She wiped her hand over the foggy windscreen and peered into the dark. "It doesn't look too deep."

Nick rested his wrist on the steering wheel and let his hand casually hang. He twisted in the seat, and the t-shirt he wore stretched across his chest, outlining toned muscles under the thin fabric. The sneer twisted on his lips was anything but casual. "How about you go out there and have a better look? There's rope in the tray if you want to tie yourself to a tree in case you get washed away."

Ava clenched her fists, tempted to punch him in his cruel face. Going back to Nick's place was out of the question. Obviously it wasn't in town or he wouldn't have suggested it.

She'd have to sleep in her car and hope for better phone reception in the morning.

"So, what's it going to be?" With intense eyes, he waited for an answer. She could tell he didn't like the second option either.

She nibbled her bottom lip. "Take me back to my car."

His eyebrows rose slightly, but he turned the truck around and headed back toward the car without any questions. His relief was palpable.

When they reached the car, she sat forward on the seat as far as the seatbelt allowed and stared with disbelief out of the windscreen. "What the hell?"

A herd of cows surrounded the vehicle. The storm

must have spooked them and they'd broken through the paddock fence. A cacophony of mooing cattle surrounded them.

Nick blasted the horn. The cows turned stunned expressions toward them, shuffled their feet, and continued with their song.

The horn blasted again, this time longer. A few shuffled away, but there was still a wall of cattle in front of the car.

They sat in silence, staring at the animals. Then Nick leaned over her, their chests colliding, and his face inches from hers. Ava sucked in a startled breath and shrieked, "What the hell are you doing?" Did he think they were going to get-it-on in his truck?

"Not what you're obviously thinking. You still have a dirty mind." His gaze dropped to her mouth, and when he raised his eyes back to met hers, a cold chill blasted from them.

"Wouldn't go there again."

Ava wanted to slap his face, but she was pinned against the seat. "There's no chance in hell I'd let you," she spat.

Nick nudged opened the passenger side door, and with a wave of his hand said, "Enjoy your evening."

The jerk was going to abandon her to deal with the cattle. Well, she'd never been scared of a few docile cows. How hard could it be to make them move?

She straightened her shoulders, jutted her chin out, and stepped into the heavy rain, thankful that the thunder and lightning had stopped. Ignoring Nick's low chuckle, she slammed the door. "I hope the stupid door falls off his shit box car," she grumbled.

She tried balancing on wobbly heels as they sank into the thickened mud. The wind whipped through her hair and the rain stung her face as the cows watched her approach with suspicion.

Waving her hands above her head, she took a few steps toward them. "Shoo! Shoo!" The cows shuffled closer to the Mercedes.

She waved her arms again, stepped closer, and threatened, "Move or I'll make hamburgers out of you!"

The cow with beady, brown eyes standing closest to Ava must not have appreciated the threat. It swung its rump in her direction, hoisted its tail high, and released a very large, very runny, cow patty all over her favorite Louis Vuitton shoes.

"Argh!" she screamed. "You dumb animal. Do you know how much they cost?"

No, of course not, it was a cow. She shook her feet, trying to flick off the muck. The cow glanced over its shoulder—Ava could have sworn it was smiling—and mooed.

"You are so going to be minced meat."

Once again it lifted its tail, but this time Ava was quick to move out of the way. But in doing so, she thumped into another cow that had sneaked up behind her, and it sent her sprawling on her hands and knees into the soggy mud. Wrinkling her nose, she didn't want to think about the cow shit mixed in.

She wanted to kick her legs and scream, but it would

only give Nick the satisfaction of watching her throw a tantrum. Being covered in mud and cow shit was enough humiliation for one night. The truck's headlights shined on her like a spotlight on a performer. He sat in his truck, warm and toasty, probably laughing his arse off while she battled the elements and livestock. He wouldn't be laughing for long when she dragged cow shit into his truck.

But the night of humiliation wasn't over. She now had the arduous task of slugging back through the mud and asking him to take her to his house. She tilted her head toward the turbulent skies, praying that the universe would send her a lifeline. The rain splattered her face as she waited. Then a cow nudged her from behind and she stumbled, catching herself before she again face-planted into the mud. She glared back at the culprit and was certain it was the same animal that did its business on her shoes. By the looks of things, the universe didn't give a crap.

The door creaked as she threw herself back inside the truck. She sat with a stiff spine and stared straight ahead. "I'll go back to your place." The words sliced her throat like razor blades.

"And you're assuming I'm still offering?"

Her head snapped around, and she shot him a glare. She ignored his disgusted perusal.

"Are you going to take me back to your place or not?"

Wrinkling his nose, he took in her disheveled state. "When a woman wants me to take her home she smells a lot sweeter."

Ava reached for the door handle to leave. She wouldn't beg. Where she would go she didn't know. Anywhere would be better than here with Nick seeing her at her worst.

The truck moved before she could make her exit. She clamped her mouth shut, and they sat in stony silence in the dim interior, the lights from the dashboard doing little to mask the repulsive mud and cow shit covering her Gucci pants and Louis Vuitton heels. She slid Nick a quick glance. His hard profile showed nothing of the boy who once found fun in everything.

Tense lines bracketed his mouth.

He turned onto a road she knew well. Did his parents still live on the cattle farm on this road? Did he live close by too?

Memories came flooding back of her traveling this same road, in the same truck, next to the same man. Those times were a lot happier. But she didn't want to think about it and pushed the memories away. Just like she'd done for the past ten years.

She glanced down at herself. God, she needed a shower. No way did she resemble the successful, put-together lawyer she was. She wiped her hands on what were once white pants. Streaks of mud and cow manure added to the blend of shades of brown from her fall. She wanted to gag.

They approached a beautiful two-story sandstone house. Nick slowed down. For a beat, she thought he was going to turn onto the horseshoe-shaped driveway, and was a little surprised to think that this elegant house might be his home. He took a long look at the lights shining through a window on the lower level, and as Ava was about to ask him if they were stopping there, he sped back up.

He drove for another few minutes until they reached a gravel driveway. The same one that led to Nick's parents' house. "Are we going to your mum and dad's place?"

"Yep."

He hadn't strung a sentence together since they'd left her car. He might not be happy being stuck with her, but she wasn't doing a happy dance either.

"Do you still live with them?" That would be strange if he did. Thirty-one years old and still living at home.

"No."

"For Christ's sake, Nick, I know you don't want me around, but would it kill you to give me more than one-word answers?"

He parked in front of a house she recognized. A bright yellow porch light shone on the familiar weatherboard walls. New white shutters had replaced the old, flaking ones, and the wrap-around timber veranda was missing the scuffs and scratches of a busy home. In its place gleamed polished timber. How many times had she walked up those steps? Too many to count.

Turning the truck off, Nick shifted in the seat to face her. "Not that I have much to say to you, but I'm not talking because I'm trying not to breathe. You fucking stink." With that, he got out of the truck fast, slammed the door behind him, and jogged to the front door, leaving her to simmer in her own stench.

Having no other choice, Ava followed. She couldn't stay in the truck smelling like garden fertilizer the whole night. She'd do anything for a hot shower. When she got out of the truck, she didn't bother rushing to the house; she couldn't get any wetter. Instead, she dawdled over the uneven ground, hoping the rain would wash away some of the muck.

When she reached the front door, Nick was already at the pot belly stove starting a fire.

Being wet down to the bone, a fire would be welcoming.

She kicked off her ruined shoes, leaving them outside. They had no chance of survival now anyway. She padded on bare feet onto the worn rug in front of the fire. She would have loved to stand in front of the warmth to defrost, but what she really needed was to be clean.

"Nick?"

"Yeah?" He didn't bother to look up at her as he crouched by the flames, stabbing it with a fire poker.

"I need to use your shower." Surely he wouldn't refuse her the use of it. Not after complaining about how bad she smelled.

"Do you remember where it is?"

"Yes."

"There are clean towels in the bathroom cupboard," he said, still not making eye contact.

Once in the small room, she took stock of her reflection in the golden framed mirror above the sink and groaned. Her hair, once glossy and full of volume, hung in damp clumps and stuck flat to her head. Chunks of things she didn't want to think about were tangled in the wet strands. The makeup she'd applied today was washed away except for the smearing of mascara streaking down her cheeks. She gave the term *panda eyes* a whole new meaning.

If only Jade and Lauren were here to see the mess she was in. They were Ava's dearest friends in the world. Meeting at university, they'd become fast friends. Their bond was as tight as sisters, and she couldn't imagine life without them. They always teased her about her immaculate appearance and how they had never seen her looking anything but perfect. They'd die of shock at the sight of her right now. Even with Nick's black jumper hanging down to her knees, she couldn't hide the caked-on mud and crap.

She sat on the edge of the bathtub. She was exhausted. Placing her elbows on her thighs, she cupped her face in her hands. The day had gone to shit...literally. But Ava had no time to feel sorry for herself. She needed to clean up, and then hopefully things wouldn't look so dismal.

She threw the disgusting clothes in a heap on the tile floor and stepped under the hot spray of the shower, moaning in ecstasy. A shower had never felt so good. She took extra care washing her hair because she wanted no nasties left behind.

Using Nick's soap to wash her body felt too personal, but she had no other choice; she needed to scrub clean. The scent of almond oil and sandalwood steamed up in the shower and images of Nick standing naked in the stall instantly filled her mind. She shivered under the warm spray. *God, why did those images have to pop up?*

She reluctantly finished, wrapped a towel around her body, and another for her hair. It was then she remembered she had left her suitcase in the car. She had no clean clothes to change into, and there was no way in hell she was putting her putrid clothes back on.

Dammit. She had to ask Nick for something again. What had she done in her life to be punished like this?

She cracked open the bathroom door and peered around it into the living room. This was silly hiding behind a door. Nick had seen her wear a lot less. Hell, she wore a lot less at the gym. Shoulders pulled back, she stepped from behind the door. She would not let Nick make her feel awkward.

Before she could call out to him and ask him for something to wear, she paused when she heard his low, deep voice. "Are you sure everything's okay?"

He stared out the front window with a phone held to his ear. His black, wavy hair, which looked in need of a trim, was still damp, but he'd changed out of the wet clothes. Faded jeans molded around his firm butt, and a white t-shirt revealed ropey arms. Warmth flushed her skin.

What the hell was wrong with her? She'd seen hotter, or at least she tried to believe her own lie.

"It's getting late. I thought you'd be in bed by now." He paused as he listened to the person on the other end. "I wanted to come by, but the storm hit and now I'm stuck with a problem."

Ava sneered. *I'm a problem?*

"It's nothing serious. Don't worry." By the soft tones he used, she could tell he was talking to a woman. Although he hadn't used that gentle tone on her all night.

"How's Molly? Did the storm scare her?" He laughed, and it surprised Ava that he still knew how. "You know my little sweetheart will hog the bed."

Molly? His little sweetheart? Did Nick have a daughter? Was he on the phone with his wife? If so, where were they?

Then, like he felt her presence, he whirled around. The smile he wore, filled with love and affection for whomever he was talking to, was beautiful, and for a second, her heart squeezed. She remembered a time when his eyes shone at her with affection. Now it dropped the moment he spotted her.

His heated gaze traveled down the length of her. Something fierce and hot flashed in his eyes, and her body burned like he'd physically stroked her. But before she could read too much into his stare, the heat fizzled out from the blue depths.

"I have to go," he said into the phone. He nodded at whatever the person said, like they could see him, and replied, "Love you too." He ended the call and shoved the phone in the back pocket of his jeans.

Ava marched into the living room, not giving away how the brief glance had affected her. She put the reaction down to the fact that it had been a long, tiring day and her guard had dropped. It meant nothing. Nick was still a jerk, and she now had to ask the jerk for another favor.

"I have nothing to wear. Do you have something I can borrow?"

He crossed his arms over his chest and leaned against the window frame. "You keep getting yourself in a predicament tonight, don't you?"

The smug smile on his arrogant face needed to be wiped off. "Well, I do like to sleep naked and tend to get up during the night if you're comfortable with that?" She slipped her fingers in the knot of her towel like she was about to let it drop.

Nick's nostrils flared, and his jaw tightened.

She couldn't suppress her smile of satisfaction. Mr. Cool wasn't so cool after all.

He sneered and stormed into what she remembered was his parents' bedroom. A couple of minutes later he reappeared with a bundle in his arms. He threw it at her. "Here, put these on."

She let go of the grip on the towel to catch the clothes. The knot loosened, and it dropped in a puddle at her feet.

They both froze for a beat. Nick's eyes were back to flashing fierce hot flames, and Ava's heart skidded to a stop as she clutched the bundle of clothes to her chest.

She was the first to break the spell. "Having a good look?"

His lip curled into a cruel sneer. "Nothing I haven't seen before." Then he spun on his heels and stormed back into the bedroom, slamming the door.

"Sweet dreams," she yelled at the closed door. She let out a shuddery breath and sank down onto the couch.

## Chapter 4

The next morning, Nick fried eggs, was on his third cup of coffee, and running on two hours of sleep.

After seeing Ava naked he had needed something to occupy his mind, and what better way to do that than to battle the elements and secure the cattle. Or so he thought. But the image of her naked body with the firelight giving her an ethereal glow was stronger than the gusts of wind and rain knocking him about. She'd matured in all the right places. Tomboyish, slim hips had grown into womanly curves. The brief glimpse of her breasts revealed they'd filled out perfectly, and her Spanish heritage gave her slender figure an all-year-round tan.

Nick threw palings, wire fencing, and a tool box into the tray of the truck and headed back to where the cows had broken through the fence. Without Molly and his dirt bike, it took him two hours to round up the scared cows back in the paddock. He did a temporary repair job on the fence as best as he could in the dark, stormy conditions and hoped it would hold until he could do a better job in the daylight.

When he finally arrived home, he found Ava asleep on the living room couch, a blanket draped over her. She'd pressed her palms together and tucked them under her cheek. The innocent pose belied her true nature.

He took a quick shower and collapsed face down on his bed, but the images of her were still scorched into his brain. Yes, he'd said her body was nothing he hadn't seen before, but he'd been lying. Although Nick had seen Ava naked many times, she'd grown into an extremely sexy woman, and *that* was an Ava he'd never seen before.

After tossing and turning, exhaustion finally hit him, and he fell asleep, only for his internal body clock to wake him up at the crack of dawn.

Ava entered the kitchen as he sat down at the small table. She wore the white t-shirt he'd given her last night minus the track pants. The hem of the shirt only just covering her arse showcased her long, toned legs.

Sitting at the table next to him, the soft fabric rode higher up her thigh, and his gaze trailed the hem. She must have noticed where Nick's attention had drifted, because she said, "Your track pants are too big."

"Coffee's still hot, and there are more eggs in the pan if you want something to eat." The tone in his voice was gruff.

She rose and made herself at home in his kitchen like she'd done so many times in the past, like nothing had changed. Then she reached into the top cupboard for a mug, and the t-shirt rode high along her thighs, and red silk underwear peeked from under the hem. He choked and coffee splatted on the table.

She turned with a questioning glance.

Nick thumped his chest. "Coffee went down the wrong way." And before she figured out the real reason he was choking, he quickly added, "Your suitcase is in the spare bedroom." He'd retrieved it when he went to repair the fence.

"Thanks." She pulled the kitchen window curtain back and peered outside.

Even from where he sat he could see the gray, dismal day. The rain fell hard at a fast, steady rate. There was no chance of crossing that road today.

She dropped the curtain back in place and carried her plate and coffee cup to the table.

"How did you get past the cows?"

"They'd moved on."

"Will I be able to get my car into town?" She sounded hopeful.

"No."

The coffee cup paused at her lips. "No?" She placed it back on the table. "You said they've moved on."

"They have."

"So, what's the problem?"

"The road is still under water."

"I can get to town if we go back to the highway," she said.

"I've got better things to do with my time than to be

your personal chauffeur. Have someone pick you up. I'm not driving in that."

He rose, scraping the chair on the timber floor, and took his empty plate to the sink. He rinsed it and put it in the dishwasher. When he turned to face her, he kept his face void of all emotions. He picked up his cap from the chair and shoved it on his head. Snatching the raincoat off a hook on the wall, he thrust his arms into the sleeves and stomped toward the back door.

"Where are you going?" she called after him.

"Out." He swung open the door without a backward glance and stepped into the morning rain.

She followed him onto the veranda. "What am I supposed to do here?"

Pausing in front of the garage, he rubbed his brow. A headache pounded behind his eyes. He blew out a frustrated breath and slowly turned around.

She stood on the veranda, hands on her hips. The light from inside the kitchen silhouetted her body underneath the white fabric of the t-shirt, and a surge of heat swamped him. Dammit, the sight of her should make him sick, not fucking turned on.

He pinched the bridge of his nose, and closed his eyes for a beat. "Make arrangements to leave?" He didn't disguise the hope in his voice.

"I probably shouldn't risk anyone driving in this."

But it was okay for him to risk his life. "As much as I love our little chitchat, my arse is getting soaking wet." He turned to go inside the garage.

"Wait!" she called, stopping him.

Dropping his head for a moment, he turned back around.

"Seriously, what am I supposed to do here?"

He threw his hands into the air. "Paint your fingernails for all I care."

"Gee, how about after I do that I strap on an apron and cook you a three-course dinner?" She clasped her hands in front of her, causing her breasts to squeeze together. Was she tormenting him on purpose?

With a will of its own, his gaze dropped to her chest. Her nipples, probably from the cool morning air and not a reaction to him, pressed against the t-shirt. He drew in a deep breath and turned to leave. "That would be great. I like to eat at six."

Ava watched him storm toward the old garage and couldn't help but admire the way his faded blue jeans fit snuggly around his firm arse and toned legs. He was a jerk but still a sexy jerk. Why couldn't he have been bald with a beer belly? When he reached the garage, he swung the door open so hard she was surprised it didn't fall off its rusty hinges.

The thought of being stuck in the house all day wasn't appealing, and he'd have a better chance of the cows making him dinner. But spending time with Nick wasn't an ideal choice either. If she went with him, perhaps she could convince him to take her back to town. The idea of calling her father to pick her up wasn't an option.

She rushed inside, passed Nick's parents' bedroom, and wondered where they were. She must remember to ask about them, they'd been like a second family. Guilt at leaving Sunland Valley without saying goodbye pressed heavy on her chest. She hoped they'd forgiven her.

Once in the spare room, she flung open her suitcase and sifted through its contents. Not exactly farm attire, but would she really wear anything that was remotely 'country' if she'd known she'd be stuck on a cattle farm? The answer was no.

She chose a pair of black, shiny jeans with silver zippers and a dark gray, silk, spaghetti strap tank top. This morning the weather was cool, so she threw on a long, caramel-colored waterfall coat. She could always take it off when the morning warmed. Choosing shoes was a problem. Jimmy Choos and another pair of Louis Vuittons were her only options. She'd already ruined a great pair last night, but unless she wanted to clunk around in a pair of Nick's work boots, she needed to select a pair to wear. She decided on the Jimmy Choos because they were a soft, leather ankle boot. *Boots are farm appropriate, aren't they?*

If she'd had time she would've applied makeup, but all she could do was a quick swipe of chili red lip gloss. She ran a brush through her hair and it fell into a straight bob. She was thankful for a great salon treatment that allowed her locks to stay straight and silky smooth.

She probably should've stayed at the house and called Isabella to let her know she'd made it to Sunland Valley. But Bella wasn't expecting her until tomorrow. She'd left a day early because she wanted to get into town and settle into the bed-and-breakfast before she faced the family.

She hurried into the kitchen and paused at the back door. Slick sheets of rain came pouring down so hard dirt bounced from the ground. Sighing, she glanced at her beautiful boots and silently said goodbye. She was also without an umbrella; last night hers went flying with the wind. She'd get soaked if she went outside. Searching around the kitchen, she spotted the weatherproof jacket Nick had worn last night. It wouldn't offer a lot of protection, but it would have to do. Instead of wearing it over her clothes, she held it high above her head and ran in the direction of the garage.

Once inside, her eyes took a moment to adjust to the dim interior. The room was filled with farming equipment, and she found Nick bent over the bonnet of his truck. The sleeves of his navy shirt were rolled to his elbows, his muscles flexing as he tinkered with the motor. She could appreciate a good-looking man, it was nothing more than that.

"What are you doing?"

His shoulders tensed for a beat then released before he answered without taking his eyes off the motor. "Checking the oil and water."

"I can't believe you still have this old truck," she said, kicking a tire.

"Nothing wrong with it."

"Do you work on the farm now?" she asked.

He made a grunting sound. She took that as a yes.

"I thought you wanted to take over Collin Benson's old mechanical workshop."

Nick shoved his fingers through his hair. "Ava, I'm busy. I don't have time to catch up on the last ten years. Nor do I want to." He slammed the bonnet shut, the sound vibrating through the shed.

Through gritted teeth, she said, "Believe me, it's not rainbows and unicorns being stuck here with you either. But it is what it is. We can at least try to be civil to one another." Even though she hated being here with Nick she could try to make it as painless as possible.

He didn't answer. Instead, he sauntered around her and got into the truck.

Dashing for the passenger side, she slid onto the seat before he could take off without her.

He slid her a long look. "What are you doing? Get out of the truck."

"No, I'm coming with you." She closed the door and arranged her coat so she could sit more comfortably.

"What happened to you cooking me a three-course meal?"

She scoffed. "Like that would really happen." She pointed to the opening of the shed.

"What are you waiting for?"

"For you to get out."

Stubbornly, she said, "Not going to happen."

"I'm going to check on fences and do repairs." His lips flattening in a stern line, the words sounded strained.

She didn't know why she was so determined to stay with him. The resentful feelings bouncing off of him and her own bitterness should have made her want to stay at the house.

Maybe it was the fact she bugged the hell out of him, which pleased her immensely. "I can help you check the fences."

His gaze swept over her, and he let out a short, harsh laugh. "You're gonna help me dressed like that?"

"I can spot the damaged ones for you from the inside of the truck."

He shook his head. "No way, Avi-baby."

Ava gasped and Nick slammed his lips shut. They both stared wide-eyed at each other at the mention of the playful nickname he'd called her when they were younger.

Clearing his throat, he broke eye contact and started the truck. "If you want to tag along, you're gonna have to help."

She didn't mention anything about her nickname. She wasn't exactly sure how she felt hearing it again after all these years. "But my outfit…"

"Is fucking ridiculous," he finished.

"I wasn't exactly planning on being stranded on a farm."

"What happened to the clothes I gave you last night?"

She let out a surprised laugh. "You don't expect me to wear your oversized track pants and t-shirt, do you?"

"It's better than what you have on."

"If I change, will you wait for me?"

"No."

She crossed her arms over her chest. "Then I'll stay dressed as I am."

He growled something she didn't quite understand, but by the tone she knew it wasn't anything pleasant.

They sat in stony silence as they drove along the gravel driveway. She was sure Nick hit every pothole and bump on purpose, bouncing her around. After hitting a particularly deep hole, Ava bounced high off the seat, landing very close to him. Reaching out to grip the edge of the seat to steady herself, her hand instead landed in Nick's lap, grabbing his crotch like a handbrake. She snatched it away as if she'd been burned. He slammed on the brakes, and the truck skidded to a stop.

A flare of heat lit up his eyes, but it was gone in a flash, replaced by a deep frown. She covered her mouth with her hand in mock surprise. She wasn't about to let him know her heart was hammering in her chest. "Oops. Sorry about that."

Hooded eyes stared at her. "Anything you want to continue with? I know I told you I didn't want to talk about old times, but I'd be happy to screw like the good ol' days."

Two could play that game. Ava slid closer, so their thighs pressed together, and trailed an index finger from his knee toward his crotch. She leaned in, making sure her breasts brushed against his arm, and whispered in his ear, "Find the nearest cluster of trees and let's see if we've still got it."

A strong hand slammed down on her exploring finger before it hit the mark, and he flicked it off his thigh. As he took off, gravel spun from the tires.

She slid closer to the passenger side door, putting as

much distance as she could between them. What was meant to cause him discomfort and put him in his place, backfired when she'd felt his hard thigh. Her body burned like fire from the inside out, and she squirmed in the seat.

She propped her elbow on the window, portraying a look of nonchalance. "Why Nick, have you suddenly grown bashful?"

Without taking his eyes off the road, he answered, "No, my standards of who I have sex with are higher these days."

She sucked in a sharp breath, but before she had time to retaliate, he continued like they were having a casual conversation about the weather.

"I have to make a stop and pick up Molly."

Ava glanced out the window. He drove into the driveway of the house they'd passed last night, her curiosity about Molly overriding Nick's insult. If Molly was his daughter, why was she here and not at the house with him? After his comment a moment ago, surely he wasn't married, but if he was, she'd personally help his wife castrate him.

Nick pinned her with a hard look. "Stay here." He got out of the truck, hunched his shoulders against the rain, and ran toward the wide, timber veranda.

"Not a chance," she muttered. Retrieving her makeshift umbrella, she held it over her head and followed.

As she reached the shelter of the veranda, Nick spun toward her, and his expression grew dark. "I told you to stay in the truck."

She met his glare with one of her own. "I don't take orders." She then grilled, "Who's Molly? Is she your daughter?"

His eyebrows rose with surprise, and he laughed. A real laugh, reminding her of the youthful, happy guy she'd once loved. No, *thought* she loved. They'd been too young for something so serious. Obviously, her assumption about Molly was wrong, but she didn't have a clue what he thought was so funny.

"Molly, come here, girl," he yelled through the screen door.

Excited barking echoed somewhere from inside the house, and the sound of tapping on timber floors came rushing toward the front door. Nick opened the screen, and a hyperactive cattle dog bounded out onto the veranda, jumping up and down in front of him, wanting his attention.

He bent down on one knee and scratched the dog under the chin. "Hey, beautiful girl, did you miss me?"

Molly answered by licking his face. He laughed and wiped off the slobber with his shoulder.

He rose and introduced the happy dog to Ava. "This is Molly."

Ava clapped her palms on her thighs to get Molly's attention, and the dog happily jumped up and put her front paws on Ava's legs, looking for more love.

"You could've told me Molly was your dog." She stroked the top of Molly's head.

"And ruin the surprise?" He clicked his fingers.

"Molly, sit." The dog left Ava and obediently sat next to his feet.

"Have that control with all women?" She snickered.

"If I did, you'd still be sitting in the truck."

She pulled a face.

"Ava, is that you?" a familiar voice called from inside the house.

Nick groaned.

"Does your mother live here?" She threw him a look.

Before Nick had a chance to answer, his mother Maggie stepped out onto the veranda. Ava's heart tripped a beat seeing her after so many years. A few extra lines creased her smooth, creamy skin and her dark brown hair had some grays scattered through it, but those were the only changes. Piercing blue eyes as bright as Nick's smiled. God, Ava had missed her.

"Oh my gosh, it is you." Maggie wrapped her in a tight hug. Ava breathed in deeply the familiar scent of vanilla and orange blossoms. Maggie pulled back, leaving her hands on Ava's shoulders. "It's so wonderful to see you. It's been so long."

"It's great seeing you too, Maggie." Nostalgia lodged in her throat. "I've missed you."

Maggie's blue eyes misted. "I've missed you too." She waved a hand in front of her face. "I'm turning into such a sook. Come inside and I'll make us a cuppa and you can tell me what's brought you back home."

Ava flinched at the word *home*, but Maggie didn't seem to notice. Why she was in Sunland Valley, she wasn't exactly sure yet until she spoke with Bella. "I'd love to catch up."

Then her gaze swept the front of the house. "Do you live here?"

"Didn't Nicky tell you?"

Ava shot Nick a glare. "He isn't exactly full of information. I'm lucky if he mutters more than two words to me."

Maggie gave her a sympathetic smile. "That's because you broke poor Nicky's heart."

* * *

"Let's go." Nick caught Ava's arm and pulled her toward the steps of the veranda. He needed to get her away before his mother said another word.

"Wait, Nick. I'd like to stay and visit with Maggie." Ava tried pulling him to a stop, but he kept moving.

"No time, we have fences to mend. See you later, Mum." He didn't even give Ava time to cover her head with the jacket she'd brought along. Nick whistled at Molly, and she followed close behind.

Ava stumbled down the stairs. "Nick, slow down!"

He didn't; he just kept pulling her toward the truck. If she'd only listened and stayed inside the truck. No, stayed at the house, so she wouldn't be staring at him with wide eyes over the bomb his mother dropped.

Ava yanked her arm free, flung open the passenger door, and threw herself inside. Normally, he would let Molly ride in the tray, but he didn't want her traveling in the rain, so he gave her a command and she leaped inside. Muddy paws landed straight on Ava's coat.

"Molly, no!" Ava cried and tried to pull it free. But Molly propped her head on top of her paws and made herself comfortable.

Ava glowered at Nick. "Do you mind getting your dog off my coat?" Then she held a finger under her nose and wrinkled it with disgust. "God, she stinks."

"Suck it up, princess." Silently, he agreed that Molly stank. Wet dog wasn't the greatest of smells. He couldn't even wind down the window, but he wasn't about to make things comfortable for Ava.

She threw her hands in the air. "You know what? Take me back to the house. Tagging along was a big mistake."

"I have too much to do to turn back. Unfortunately, we're stuck together."

Folding her arms across her chest, she blew out a breath and looked out the passenger side window. After a few moments of silence, she turned to face him. "What did Maggie mean when she said I broke your heart?"

He clenched his jaw shut. Was it too much to hope she wouldn't mention it?

"Why did she say that, Nick? I couldn't have broken your heart. You didn't love me."

He let out a short, harsh laugh. "You were always too…"

When he didn't finish the sentence, Ava swiveled her head to stare at him. "I was always too…what? I can't wait to hear it."

"You were always too busy planning your big escape to notice." He stopped the truck. "We're here."

She followed him outside, carrying the stupid jacket above her head that did nothing to protect her from the rain. Unaware of the tension surrounding her, Molly danced with excitement around their legs.

Knocking him on the shoulder to get his attention, Ava said, "Nick, you didn't love me." Her eyes narrowed like she was probing for the truth.

Ignoring her, he spun away and pulled a roll of fencing wire from the truck and hooked it over his shoulder. Next, he hoisted out a battered toolbox and marched over to the fence.

Ava trailed after him unsteadily as her heels sank into the mud. She let go of the jacket with one hand long enough to tug at his sleeve, pulling him around to face her again. Anger had replaced her skepticism. "You can't imply you loved me and leave it at that. You don't expect me to believe you had such strong feelings?"

The wire and tool box he held dropped to the ground. Couldn't she just let this go? The past was well and truly buried. He'd spent years digging the hole. He stomped along the fence line, inspecting last night's repair.

"Will you stop for a minute?" she snapped.

Nick had the impression she wanted to stamp her foot like a spoiled brat, but her heels were stuck too deep in the mud. Frustrated, he heaved a heavy sigh. "I have a lot to check on today, and it will take twice as long in this weather. Can we save this conversation for another time?" Or never if he had his way.

"The sooner you explain what Maggie meant, the sooner you can go back to being Old MacDonald. Did you love me?"

"No, I didn't love you," he lied.

A heavy sigh escaped her lips, and she nodded. "Good. That's great. Because how ridiculous would that have been? So crazy. We were so young. I don't know why Maggie thought—"

He couldn't listen to another word and trudged toward her until they were inches apart, cupping her face in his hands. Her eyes widened just before he kissed her.

## Chapter 5

For a beat, Ava's body stiffened against Nick and then melded against his chest. The jacket she'd held above her head to protect her from the rain dropped on the ground when she wrapped her arms around his shoulders, knocking the cap off his head in the process.

He pulled her closer, fusing their mouths and bodies together, drinking her in like he'd been in a drought. Hot, fast, and hungry. Kisses that had once been young and playful had matured into something deeper and more ardent.

Digging her fingers into his rain-soaked hair, she shuddered against his body. Heat slammed into him, and he vibrated with desire.

And as quickly as it started she pulled away and stumbled a step back. Her chest heaved as she sucked in deep, shuddering breaths, her eyes wide with shock.

He took a couple of rough breaths to fill his own

oxygen-deprived lungs and probably mirrored her exact same expression.

"Look at that, just like old times. 'Cept I used to catch you two locking lips in the hay shed."

Nick and Ava swung toward the interrupting voice and found Percy, Nick's farm manager, parked next to them. He hadn't heard the truck pull up, and by the surprised expression on Ava's face, she hadn't either. He used the distraction to close his eyes for a moment and take a few steady breaths to settle his hammering heart. Shit! Alone together for five minutes and she was fucking with his mind.

"Percy?" Ava, now thoroughly soaked through and not bothering with the discarded jacket, ran as best as she could in her stupid heels over to the old man who sat in the truck with the window down.

Nick's father had hired Percy to be farm manager when he bought land to start his cattle farm twenty-eight years ago. For as long as Nick could remember, Percy had looked the same. With his tanned, weathered face, salt-and-pepper hair, and tall, lanky frame, Nick didn't know if he was fifty or one hundred and fifty.

Ava leaned through the opened window and kissed him on the cheek. "It's so good to see you, and looking as handsome as ever."

"I never thought I'd see you back on the farm again. And it didn't take the two of you long to pick up where you left off."

"No, it's not what you think," Ava tried to explain.

"You were the best thing to happen to Nick. What an idiot he was for lettin' you go."

"Percy!" Nick barked. "Have you checked the top paddocks?"

At Nick's harsh tone, Percy slid a confused look between Nick and Ava.

"I sent Kev there." Nick gathered his equipment and threw it in the back of the truck. "I'll see if he needs a hand. I repaired these fences last night, double check them, the tension of the wire could be tighter. And take Ava back to the house when you're done." He avoided looking at her as he drove away.

Mud flung out from the back of Nick's tires as he sped off.

"Coward!" Ava yelled after him, not caring that Percy was watching her with curious eyes. How could Nick kiss her in a way that made the earth shake then drive away? And why the hell did he kiss her in the first place?

"Ava, get in the truck before you drown in this rain." Percy's voice snapped her back to reality.

The rain had eased a little since she'd left the house, but it still drenched through to her skin. She shivered and climbed inside Percy's truck. He'd cranked the heater on high, and she was grateful for the measly warmth it provided.

"I'll take you back to the house now before you shrivel into a prune."

"What about checking the fences?"

"They'll keep. I'll be back soon enough," he said as he navigated through the muddy paddock.

"It's so wonderful to see you, Percy."

Percy flicked her a pleased grin. "It's good to see you too, sweetheart. It's been too long."

Once more she found herself wringing out water from her hair after being caught in the pouring rain. Would she ever be dry again?

"Time got away from me." Even to her own ears her excuse sounded insincere. She'd left Sunland Valley with no intention of ever returning.

"Looks like you and Nick were making up for some lost time." He winked and then laughed when she scowled. "You don't look too happy about it."

"I'm feeling a lot of things about Nick at the moment, but *happy* isn't one of them."

Percy shook his head and made a tsking sound. "I always thought the two of you were made for each other."

"We were too young." And Nick had destroyed any hope for a future together.

Percy shrugged. "Maybe, but you two had something special. Sometimes life throws you a second chance. It's up to you whether you want to leap high enough to catch it."

"I'm not here for second chances. I don't know what that kiss was about, but it wasn't a let's-pick-up-where-we-left-off kiss."

Their relationship hadn't worked in the past, and it wasn't going to work now. She didn't want happily-ever-after. Ava dated men who knew it would only be physical—not a relationship.

She enjoyed sex and wouldn't be ashamed of it, but that's as far as it went.

Firsthand she'd witnessed what a relationship had done to her mother. How her father treated her with no respect. Parading numerous affairs in her mother's face while she ignored them but let it fester inside.

When they were about to drive past Maggie's house, she asked Percy to pull into the driveway.

"Nick told me to take you to the house."

"I'm a big girl, Percy, I can go wherever I like. Thanks for the lift."

He stopped and she gave him a quick peck on his weathered cheek, got out of the truck, and ran to the veranda.

If Maggie was surprised to find Ava back soaking wet and covered in muddy paw prints, she didn't show it. She glanced past Ava at Percy's truck driving away. "Get inside. You're soaking wet. I thought you were with Nick?"

"He had some things he needed to do."

With a silent look of skepticism, Maggie ushered her in the house and led her down the hall into a modern, with splashes of country charm, bathroom.

Maggie pulled out two fluffy rose-colored towels from the bathroom vanity and placed them on the rim of the bathtub. "Have a shower and warm up. I'll find something for you to wear, and I'll leave the clothes by the door. We'll have tea in the kitchen when you're done." She smiled and closed the door behind her.

Ava once again found herself in someone else's bathroom looking like a drowned rat and in need of something to wear. She couldn't recall ever being so disheveled in her life and now in two days she was at her absolute worst.

When she'd finished showering she wrapped a towel around her and gathered the clothes Maggie had left outside the door. She put on the soft denim jeans and secured the loose waistband with the belt Maggie provided. Ava had to forgo her bra and undies as they were too wet to put back on. The navy top was a little snug and pulled across her chest, but there wasn't much she could do about it.

Ava bundled her clothes together, careful not to drip water on the floor, and went searching for the kitchen. Walking down a hallway, she paused in front of a display of photographs framed in glossy, black timber and arranged neatly in rows along the wall. She recognized the farm. There were photos of animals, flowers, orchard trees budding with spring blossoms and others heavy with fruit. There was even one of Percy shoveling hay from the back of an ute to a herd of hungry cattle.

She looked at a photograph of Nick, his brother Brad, and their father Paul. The three of them had their arms slung over each other's shoulders, green pastures of the farm in the background. With their faces covered in dust, they looked at each other with laughing smiles. Nick's lit up face reminded her of a time when he smiled so easily.

Now, in the last few hours they'd spent together, he'd been nothing but brooding and unsmiling.

She stared at the next photo. A dilapidated, white gazebo was nestled in a clump of pine trees with wildflowers tangled amongst the tall grass. The black-and-white photo was eerily beautiful. In its former glory, she'd spent many hours sitting in the gazebo with Nick, talking, making out, and eventually making love to him for the first time. It was their place to sneak away from the rest of the world. A knot formed in the pit of her belly at the flaking paint and rotting timber. Now it looked as depleted as their relationship.

With a heavy heart, Ava continued on and found the kitchen. Maggie was getting cups ready for tea.

"Do you have something I can put my wet clothes in?"

"Give them to me. I'll toss them in the washing machine." Maggie took them from her.

"No, I don't want to bother you with them."

"It's no bother. I'll be back in a minute."

While waiting for Maggie she looked around the kitchen. It was a lot bigger than the old house Nick was living in, with sparkly, new appliances. But the smell was so familiar of the days she'd have tea with Maggie and eat whatever she'd baked that day. Scents of cinnamon and lemon tickled her nose, and nostalgia stirred in her heart.

Maggie returned. "I hope I don't ruin your clothes. They look too fancy to be washed in a machine."

Ava waved a hand. "I think they're already ruined. I doubt you could do worse."

Maggie laughed, poured the tea, and brought the steaming mugs to the table. "It's so lovely to see you again. What brings you back?"

Ava took a moment and sipped her tea, so thankful Maggie didn't hate her for leaving, and gathered her thoughts.

Maggie must have thought Ava didn't want to answer the question and quickly added, "Sorry, I didn't mean to be nosy."

"You're not being nosy. I'm here to see Bella. I'm on the farm staying with Nick because I broke down in the storm last night and he found me. He was kind enough to offer me a place to stay." More like didn't have much choice.

If Maggie had questions as to whether there was anything going on between them again, she didn't ask. Instead she said, "Your dad will be thrilled to have you home." Ava shrugged. She doubted it.

"You're still not getting along with Bernie?"

"Not exactly."

Concern lined Maggie's brow. "I would have hoped after all these years you two could have worked out your differences."

"Too much has happened."

Maggie reached out and patted her hand, giving her an understanding smile. She probably noticed Ava was uncomfortable talking about her father, because she changed the subject. "So tell me, what have you been up to all these years?"

"We could be here all night." Ava laughed, thankful Maggie had let the subject drop.

Leaning back in her chair, Maggie smiled. "I'm not going anywhere."

Ava told her about starting university straight after leaving Sunland Valley. The years of study and the horrible part-time jobs she had to endure to pay her way. She told Maggie about her friends Jade and Lauren and about their Tuesday night drinks ritual. She could see the pride in Maggie's face when she told her she'd graduated with high distinctions and was now a partner in a law firm.

"You haven't mentioned anyone special. Are you seeing anyone?" Maggie asked.

There was no one special in her life. Once she believed Nick was the special person in her life, but she'd been wrong.

"No, I'm not seeing anyone." She smiled at Maggie to reassure her she was okay with that, then added, "I'm too busy for anything serious." And basically, never would do *serious*. But Maggie didn't need to know that her parents' train wreck of a marriage twisted her views on relationships and she wanted to avoid them.

She had been at Maggie's house for over an hour and there'd been no sign of Paul. She hadn't seen him on the farm either, and wondered if he was away. "How's Paul? I haven't seen him around."

Maggie paled, and she bit her trembling bottom lip. Icy fingers crawled up Ava's spine, and she wished she'd never asked the question, because now she really didn't want to know the answer.

"Nicky didn't tell you?" Maggie's voice cracked.

Ava shook her head, not trusting her voice to sound any clearer, and waited with dread for what was to come.

"Paul died almost seven months ago. He had a heart attack. Percy found him in the west paddock, but there was nothing he could do." Maggie wiped a tear from her cheek.

"Oh, Maggie." Ava rose from the chair, knelt in front of the grieving woman, and hugged her. "Why did you let me carry on about the stupid things happening in my life? I feel like an insensitive cow." The sadness of Paul's death tore at her heart.

Maggie cupped Ava's face, kissed her on the cheek, and smiled warmly. "Not stupid,

Ava, a life to be proud of."

Ava sat back down. She couldn't believe Nick never told her about Paul. She wanted to be angry at him for keeping it from her, but she knew talking about the death of his father wouldn't be easy. He barely spoke to her at all, so he wouldn't want to talk about something so painful.

"How are you coping?"

"I won't lie, it's been tough. I keep expecting him to walk through the door at any minute, dragging mud all over my floors." Maggie brushed away another tear.

Ava could only imagine how hard it must be for her. Maggie and Paul's marriage was the real deal. When she'd met Nick's parents, she'd held on to a small amount of hope that true love really existed. And once thought she might have found it with Nick before things went wrong.

"I'm so sorry. Paul was a wonderful man." She squeezed Maggie's hand.

"Thank you," Maggie said, squeezing back. She shook her head and waved a hand. "Enough depressing talk. We need something stronger to drink than tea. I have a nice bottle of Shiraz we should open." She rose and rummaged inside a cupboard.

Ava glanced at the digital time on the microwave and laughed. "It's only eleven in the morning."

Maggie paused with the bottle in her hand. "It is?" She shrugged. "We can have an early lunch. I have some leftover pasta salad if that's okay with you?"

"You don't need to feed me." Maggie never let her leave with an empty stomach.

"I know I don't. I want to." She pointed in the direction she'd left earlier with her wet clothes. "While I get lunch ready, would you mind putting your clothes in the dryer? I heard the washing machine stop."

"Sure." Ava went in search of the laundry and put the clothes in the dryer.

Back in the kitchen, Maggie had pasta salad, sliced crusty, thick bread, and wine set on the table.

"This looks delicious." She sat down, scooped the pasta onto her plate, and buttered a slice of bread.

"Eat up. There's plenty left over. I made it for Nicky last night, but he never made it to dinner." She frowned. "He never mentioned it was you he was helping."

"Honestly, I think he wished he'd never stopped to

help." Ava shrugged. "We're both a bit touchy around each other."

Maggie blotted the side of her mouth with a napkin. "I'm not exactly sure what happened between the two of you all those years ago, but I do remember how in love you were. And then all of a sudden you left without uttering a word, leaving poor Nicky heartbroken."

It was the second time Maggie had mentioned Nick's broken heart. For Ava to have broken it, he needed to have one to start with. Nothing warm beat in the cold, dark cave in his chest.

Maggie continued. "He hid it well. Then when the rumor circulated about Nicky and Bradley opening a brothel in town, he disguised his hurt with anger."

Ava knew Maggie was wrong. If he'd been angry, it was because the link to her father's money left town, not because of a broken heart. He told her himself he never loved her.

"Starting the rumor about the brothel was definitely childish. I never should have done that," Ava admitted, but at the time it was the only thing she could think of to hit Nick where it hurt. And it wasn't his heart.

"We all do silly things when we're hurt. Often lash out at the ones we love the most." Maggie was always so forgiving. Unlike Nick.

And after ten years, he was still mad. Actually, he only looked mad when he offered her a place to stay; afterward, he'd showed her nothing but cold indifference. Except for when he'd kissed her earlier...there'd been nothing cold and unfeeling about that. She didn't know why he did it, but she didn't want to think about it right now, because if she did, she'd remember that when their lips met, heat surged through every nerve of her body. And this wasn't the time or place to relive it.

They finished their meal and washed the dishes. Maggie gathered the wine glasses and Ava followed her out of the kitchen with the bottle. They entered the hall of pictures. "I absolutely love these photos. Who's the photographer?"

"I took them." Maggie blushed at the compliment.

"You did? Maggie, they're so beautiful. I never knew you were into photography." Maggie had captured the heart and soul of the farm and the people who worked it beautifully.

Ava was impressed.

"Nicky bought me a camera for Christmas a couple of years ago and I went trigger happy." She laughed. "Everyone was sick of me pointing the camera in their faces, so I took photos of the land and animals because they couldn't complain. And the farm is always changing and giving me plenty of material to work with." She smiled lovingly at the photo of Paul with his arms around his two boys. "That was the last photo I took of the three of them together. It's not often they're on the farm at the same time. They didn't even know I'd taken it until I hung it on the wall."

Ava put her arm around Maggie's shoulders. "It's a beautiful shot. You can see so much love."

"The boys miss him." Maggie's voice cracked, and Ava pulled her tighter. She knew the pain of losing a parent.

Even though Ava's mother had battled demons, not realizing the effect it had on her young daughter, she never doubted her love.

To lighten the mood, she said, "Maggie, these photos are good enough to sell. I know a few artsy-fartsy people who would love a bit of rustic chic in their city offices or homes. My best friend Lauren has a homewares shop, and I bet she would love these." Ava's eyes were again drawn to the dilapidated gazebo. "I would love to hang one in my place too." "I've already sold lots of them on eBay." Maggie grinned.

Ava gasped with surprise. "You have? That's wonderful!"

"I can't believe what people are paying for them. I feel a little guilty."

Ava laughed. "There's nothing to feel guilty about. You should be so proud of your talent."

Maggie dipped her head. "It's only a hobby, but now that I have more time on my hands I thought I'd see how they'd sell." Her eyes sparkled as she smiled. "Apparently very well." They laughed as they continued on into the living room.

Maggie's house was a big transformation from the modest one where Nick now lived. Each room she'd seen was filled with lush furniture and expensive appliances. All decorated with a contemporary feel and a touch of country charm. It made her happy to see that Paul must have turned the farm into a profitable business. Ava knew there had been a time that they had struggled financially.

"Your house is beautiful. Have you been here long?" she asked.

Maggie refilled their glasses, then tucked her legs up on the couch. "It's coming onto five years. It was always too big for Paul and me, but Nicky insisted we needed a new house. I thought it was a waste of his money. We were happy with our little cottage."

Nick's money? "Nick bought you this house?" How could he afford a house like this? He was still living at his parents' old one and drove the same truck he did ten years ago.

Just then Nick entered the room, and her eyes collided with his iceberg glare. "Dad paid for the house with years of sweat and blood."

$\mathcal{N}$ick should've known he wouldn't find Ava back at the house, and he definitely knew she wouldn't be in the kitchen preparing a three-course meal.

After driving around the farm for longer than necessary, he'd come to the conclusion there wasn't much he could do in this weather, went back to the house, and found it empty. Only the smell of Ava's perfume lingered in the air. The same sweet scent that had clung to him all day after he'd kissed her.

Was he insane? He'd wanted to shut that sexy mouth, stop her from dragging up the past. But if he were to be honest, tasting her again was all he could think about, and it was driving him crazy. If Percy hadn't shown up, would they have taken it further? Ava may have pulled away, but desire shone bright from her eyes.

The interruption was like a splash of ice water in the face. It shook him out of the lust haze he'd been trapped in. He hadn't been with her twenty-four hours and he was ready to ignore the misery she'd left behind. How could he forget, even for a second, the way she'd screwed him over?

Now seeing her settled comfortably with his mother like she was part of his life again caused a vein to pulse at the side of his head. His fist clenched. She hadn't just left Nick, she'd left his parents too. And now she thought she could slide right back in? Like hell!

"Nicky, I didn't hear you come in. Have you finished for the day?" His mother smiled brightly.

"There's not much more I can do in the rain." His eyes narrowed at Ava. "What are you doing here? You were supposed to be at the house."

She glowered back. "I wanted to visit with Maggie."

The vein in his head throbbed like a jackhammer. Then his gaze dropped to her outfit and another head began to throb. A tight, navy t-shirt stretched across her chest like a second skin, and it was obvious she wasn't wearing a bra.

"What the hell are you wearing?" he asked.

"Maggie was kind enough to lend me her clothes while mine dried." She tilted her chin like she was daring him to say something more, but his brain couldn't form any words.

Probably sensing the tension between them or just noticing the deathly glares they were firing at each other like daggers, his mother rose from the couch and looped her arm through his. "Come in the kitchen and help me make coffee." And to Ava, she said, "We'll be back in a few minutes."

Once in the kitchen she spun around and faced Nick. "What is your problem?"

The number one problem was sitting in the living room. "I don't know what you're talking about, but I'm sure you'll tell me." He leaned his hip on the kitchen counter, folded his arms across his chest, and waited for her to continue.

"I know you and Ava have had some differences in the past, but there's no need to be rude."

Nick blew out a long breath. "I've barely spoken to her."

"Exactly! And with the few words you have said, it's like you want to bite her head off. I didn't raise you to treat people that way."

Why was she defending Ava? "Have you forgotten how she left? What she'd nearly done to mine and Brad's business?" He shoved away from the counter and threw up his hands. "*And* she left without a word, not even a goodbye…to you," he quickly added. He didn't care anymore that she'd left him, but he remembered how hurt his parents had been, especially his mother.

They'd opened their home to Ava.

His mother placed a hand on his arm. "We don't know what made her leave or why she started that rumor. I'm sure she had a good reason. Maybe now's your chance to find out."

He couldn't believe how forgiving his mother was. Actually, what was he thinking? Of course he could believe it. How many times had she forgiven the stupid things he and Brad got caught doing? She had been a saint putting up with the two of them. She'd always blister their ears with a lecture on being responsible young men, but at the end of the day, all would be forgiven.

"I don't give a shit anymore." He frowned.

His mother raised an eyebrow. Nick was thirty-one, but she only had to give him *the look* and he was twelve years old again.

"I just want this rain to stop so she can take off." Maybe it was worth the risk driving in this weather now that there wasn't much more he could do on the farm.

"You're telling me one thing, but I know you, Nicky, you're feeling something else." She placed her hand on his chest—over his heart.

He scowled at his mother's meaning. "The only thing I'm feeling is frustration that she's still here."

And frustration of another kind, one he'd have to take care of himself since he hadn't gotten any in a while. Spending so much time on the farm or workshop hadn't given him the opportunity. Maybe that was why Ava was so tempting. *Yeah, right.* He didn't believe his own bullshit.

"I'm going to pass on the coffee." He bent down and kissed his mother's cheek. "Since I can't do much outside I'm going to catch up on the paperwork."

She caught his arm to stop him from leaving. "You're doing too much. You can't run your own company and the farm. And did I hear you were working at the workshop again yesterday?"

"Ben was busy, so I gave him a hand. Brad has everything under control with the business. You need me here."

His mother bit her bottom lip. "We can always sell."

Nick's chest tightened. "This is your home. Dad loved this place. We're not going to sell.

I'll work something out." He pulled his mother in for a hug.

When they reached Nick's house, Ava closed herself in her room. The rain still hadn't stopped, and she felt as dreary as the overcast sky and needed to be as far away from Nick as possible. And from the looks of his scowling face, the feeling was mutual.

It was time to call Bella. She pulled her phone out of her bag and dialed her sister's number.

"Ava!" Bella answered on the first ring. "You better not tell me you're not coming." She could hear the disappointment in her sister's voice.

"There's been a bit of a delay."

"You're still coming, right?"

"Yes, but I'm not sure when. Woodlands Road is flooded."

There was silence for a beat. Ava could picture Bella tugging at the ends of her long, dark brown hair. The only thing they both inherited from their father. Bella's fair skin and blue eyes were just like Bella's mother's—Ava's stepmother—while Ava's Spanish complexion was like her father's.

"Why didn't you take the highway?"

In hindsight she should've stayed on the highway, but

even though the memories in Sunland Valley weren't all great, she always loved the beautiful countryside through the back way. "The drive's so pretty."

"But why the delay? Can't you get back on the highway?"

"My car broke down." And Nick was too busy to take her. You'd think he'd want to get rid of her fast.

"Oh, that sucks. So, where are you?"

"I'm staying at a…friend's house." She nearly choked on the word *friend*.

"What friend?"

She could make up some name and Bella would never know, but she didn't want to lie to her sister. "His name is Nick Williams."

"You're staying with Nick!" Her voice rose to a squeal. "Oh my God, he's so hot. You never told me you knew him. Wait until I tell my friends at school. They're all totally crushing on him."

Ava had to laugh. She could admit Nick was good to look at, and she couldn't blame the girls for noticing.

"Are you two like hooking-up friends?" Bella asked with a giggle.

"Bella! What do you even know about *hooking-up friends*? Wait…don't answer that, I don't want to know." God, when did Isabella grow up? Being away from her had been the hardest part about moving. Ava had missed a lot. "I'll call you again tomorrow. Hopefully the rain will stop, and I can come and see you."

"Okay, and have fun with *N-i-c-k*," she said, dragging out his name.

Ava shook her head. "Bye, Bella."

She hung up, flung herself on the bed, and stared up at the ceiling. Immediately, Nick's face filled her mind, and she couldn't help but replay the morning's kiss. She was torn between wanting to slap him for kissing her and never wanting it to end. That's what annoyed her the most. She'd liked it too much, and Nick, after they broke apart, stared at her with contempt, like the thought of what they'd done sickened him.

She sprung off the bed and dressed in the oversized t-shirt Nick had given her to sleep in.

It was still early to dress for bed, but her clothing options were limited. She needed to be careful with her wardrobe until she found a dry cleaner.

Why did Maggie say she'd broken Nick's heart? He'd told her himself he didn't love her. Of course he didn't, except back then she thought he did. He'd never said the words, but the way he used to look at her… It set her heart racing. But she'd just been a kid, what had she known about love? He couldn't have done what he did if he really felt something close to love.

When he kissed her today she could have sworn, for a second, she'd seen the old Nick shining out from his eyes. Like he wanted no one but her. But hadn't she seen that look in a dozen guys' eyes? It was nothing more than desire. And now Nick wanted to pretend he hadn't felt a damn thing, not even a twinge of lust. Well, she was going to call his bluff.

She threw open her bedroom door and stormed into the dining room. Nick sat at the table surrounded with papers. He lifted his head and watched her approach with a wary expression.

"Don't pretend you didn't feel anything when we kissed." She placed her hands on her hips, pulling the t-shirt across her chest. His gaze fell to her unbound breasts and heat flashed in his eyes. Bingo!

"I didn't." His attention went back to the work on the table.

Ava didn't like being dismissed. She had a bone to pick and wanted to prove a point.

With a throaty, sexy voice, one that she'd perfected and knew worked on all men, she said, "Prove it. Kiss me again."

$$\text{———————————————}$$

Chapter 7

$$\text{———————————————}$$

 *N*ick was doing paperwork, trying unsuccessfully to forget about Ava, when she came storming out of her room, looking ready for a fight. The last thing he'd expected her to say was *kiss me again*. If she'd said they were being ambushed by big, pink, fluffy bunnies, he would have believed that more.

While she waited for an answer, she pinned him with a long, serious look. He put down his pen and leaned back in the chair. "You want me to kiss you again?" She gave a brisk nod.

"What the hell for?" Was this some kind of trick?

"To prove a point."

He blew out a breath. "A point—"

"Yes." She glared at him like he should've known what she was talking about.

"And the point being?" He waved his hand for her to explain.

She leaned her hip against the table. "The point being

that you act like I'm crap under your shoe, but I know there was something behind that kiss."

There was no doubt he felt something after the kiss. With her body pressed up against his, he'd felt the biggest hard-on he'd had in years.

"I shouldn't have kissed you. It was a mistake, so why the hell would I want to do it again?" He rose from the chair, needing to put distance between them so he wasn't tempted to make another *mistake*.

Ava pushed away from the table, blocking his path, and arched a dark eyebrow. "It may have been a mistake, but I know you were into it."

And from the way she'd responded he wasn't the only one who was into it.

Whatever she was up to needed to stop. Nick needed to spin this around until she capitulated. He stepped closer. She stepped back, and her arse bumped the table. Their chests only inches apart. She held her chin high, daring him with heated toffee eyes to do what she'd asked. He had to give it to her, she wasn't backing down. And neither would he. It was time to ramp it up.

He trailed a finger along her jaw and over her plump mouth. A mouth he'd been

obsessing over ever since he tasted her today. But if he was honest, since they first locked eyes at Dexter's.

She quivered, and her bravado slipped. Any second now she'd put a stop to this madness.

She despised him. Why would she really want to go through with this just to prove a point?

Then her gaze dropped to his mouth and her tongue

darted out to lick her bottom lip, and his mouth went dry. She was doing a great job tempting him. His willpower was flying out the window.

Groaning, he cupped her face in his hands. "I know I'm going to regret this," he mumbled as their lips collided.

Her body stiffened for a beat as if surprised he actually went through with it, then she pressed herself against his chest. A quick thought entered his mind to stop, but when she wrapped her arms around his neck and sighed into his mouth, it left just as fast. There was no way he could step away. This was meant to be a dare, and somehow, he'd failed miserably.

Pulling her closer, Nick placed his hands under her arse and boosted her onto the dining table. She automatically wrapped her legs around his waist, gasping when the evidence of how much he wanted her rubbed against her sweet spot. Dipping his head, he trailed his mouth along her jaw and down the side of her neck. Her pulse beat at a rapid pace against his tongue. He'd forgotten how good Ava's sweet skin tasted, and he needed to have more. Like he'd been starved from his favorite food for too long, and now that he'd gotten a bite, it was all he craved.

He slid his hands down to her breasts. She sucked in a sharp breath and arched her back, her nipples peaking under his palm. Replacing his hand with his mouth, the soft fabric of her shirt frustratingly acted as a barrier to what he really wanted. And like she could read his thoughts, she lifted the hem of the t-shirt, pulled it over her head, and dropped it on the floor.

"God, you're still so beautiful. No…more so." The need for her was evident in the sound of his husky voice.

Then she slid her hands between their bodies and cupped him through his jeans.

"Oh *fuck*," he gasped, and dropped his head onto her shoulder.

She stroked her hand along the length of him, and his knees buckled. God, it felt good.

But if she continued, he'd embarrass himself in a matter of seconds.

Growling, he wrapped his fingers around her wrist and pulled her hand away. She glanced up at him with a smile that could only be interpreted as smug. Yeah, he had no doubt she knew the torture she was putting him through. But he'd put the lusty desire in her eyes too, so she wasn't getting off so lightly. And if they kept going the way they were, they'd both be 'getting off'.

But it wasn't what he'd planned. He'd wanted to call Ava's bluff and throw a spanner into her crazy idea. But instead, she was nearly bare-arsed naked, perched on top of last month's hay invoice. And as much as he hated to admit it, he wanted to finish what they'd started. It didn't matter that she'd once crushed his heart, even though he'd told her differently. Nor that it took him years to get her out of his system. His body took over his mind, and he wanted to be buried deep inside her.

As she rocked herself against him, urging him to take it further, she was back to making him want her like he'd never wanted any other woman in his life. And that's when his brain finally stepped up and took over from his body. Reminding him he'd be damned if he let himself go there again.

Abruptly, he broke away, turned his back to her, and blew out a ragged breath. "You got your kiss." And he got a raging hard-on.

Once he got his shit together he turned back and the sight of her slammed into him. She hadn't bothered putting the t-shirt back on. She leaned back with her hands behind her on the table, legs crossed at the knee, looking as confident and comfortable as if she were fully dressed.

A satisfied smile told him she'd gotten him exactly where she wanted.

"I think I got a lot more than a kiss," she said as she swung her leg back and forth.

Nick snatched the t-shirt from off the floor and threw it at her. She caught it, taking her time putting it back on.

"Yeah, you did, and a couple minutes more we would have screwed. Would that have made you happy?" Anger for succumbing so easily clutched his chest.

She slid off the table, littering the floor with papers. She stormed over to him with her head held high. "We would never have screwed. I had complete control." Her eyes darted away for a beat. She didn't fool him.

She went to march past him, but he gripped her wrist and pulled her back so their chests were touching. Her breathing came out in choppy gasps, and even though her rage was spitting out from her eyes, her body molded along his.

His lips hovered above her mouth. "Sure, tell yourself

that if it helps you sleep at night. But trust me, *I* was the one with the control. You should be thanking me for stopping."

Wildfire shot from her glare, and he was tempted to do something stupid like kiss her again when someone behind him cleared their throat.

They broke apart and whirled toward the intruder.

"Arrh, the door was unlocked, so I let myself in." His brother Brad was standing in front of the door with a huge shit-eating grin. "Mum told me I'd find you both here, but she told me I'd be walking into world war three. It appears to me more like love and war."

Nick sneered at Brad, which only made him laugh. Then he gave Ava a once-over, not a checking-her-out look, but one of disbelief, like he couldn't believe who he was seeing. Brad held his arms out wide, and Ava went rushing into them. He picked her up and spun her around, and she tilted her head back and laughed.

What the hell? Brad hated her as much as he did. They'd spent the first week after she'd left drunk at Dexter's, listing all the reasons why he'd be better off without her. When Nick finally sobered up, he'd stopped mentioning her name, and Brad never brought her up again.

His reaction at seeing Ava was like a punch in the gut. First his mother and now Brad.

The family was full of traitors.

"Brad!" he barked. Brad put Ava back on her feet but kept an arm slung over her shoulders. "What are you doing here?" *And acting overly enthusiastic with the enemy,* he wanted to add.

"Can't I drop in to see my brother? Although, I wasn't expecting it to be raining so hard or I would've reconsidered. But I risked my damn life to haul your arse back to —" "Let's grab a beer." Nick stopped him before he could finish.

He knew Brad wanted him in Sydney and back at work. But he wasn't ready for Ava to learn he wasn't a farmer. He still wanted to keep his real job to himself. Maybe it was because he hadn't been good enough for her when he'd been broke, and didn't want her changing her opinion of him because he now had money.

He glanced at Ava. The smile she had upon seeing Brad dropped like a heavy stone when she glared back at him. Obviously, she realized that he hadn't included her in the drink invitation.

"I'll leave you two boys alone. It was great seeing you again, Brad."

Nick couldn't help admiring the view as she sashayed into her room, closing the door behind her. Temptation clawed at his gut to follow her.

"She's back." Brad nudged Nick in the ribs with his elbow.

"No shit, Sherlock."

Brad laughed. "You've picked up where you left off?"

"No." Nick made his way to the kitchen, and Brad followed. He went to the fridge and pulled out two Coronas, handing one to Brad.

Brad scratched the top of his head, then he wiggled

his eyebrows. "It looked like the two of you were ready to jump each other's bones." He was two years older than Nick with a wife and a baby on the way, but he often acted like a fifteen-year-old boy.

Nick pulled back on his beer then said, "Are you going to tell me why you're here?" Although he could guess...he wanted him back at work.

Brad raised an eyebrow at the harsh tone. "Aren't you happy to see me?" He shook his head and grinned. "I guess not, I've stopped you from getting some action."

"Grow up."

"I can always go back to Mum's place if you want to finish what you started." He sniggered into his beer.

"No!" Nick practically shouted. He wasn't stupid enough to take things further with Ava, and after the dirty glares directed at him, he didn't think he'd have much of a chance even if he wanted to. But having Brad stay would be added precaution.

Brad slapped him on the back then sat in the chair at the kitchen counter. "She's back for five minutes and she's already got you all twisted."

Nick scrubbed a hand over his eyes. "She hasn't gotten me twisted."

"No? From what I witnessed, you either want to strangle her or toss her over your shoulder and take her to the nearest bedroom." He shrugged. "That's pretty twisted if you ask me. But damn, how she's grown. She was gorgeous ten years ago, but she's stunning now. It's understandable she's messing with your head."

Nick knew that this was nothing more than an observation. Brad was madly in love with his wife Lexi. A marriage Nick envied and thought he could have for himself when he'd married Kate. But he'd made a huge mistake, knew it the second he'd said "I do". He'd hated himself when he couldn't give Kate the love she deserved. It killed him to witness her devastation when it all fell apart. He'd been selfish trying to fill a gap caused by another woman.

Then Nick remembered how excited Brad had been seeing Ava and betrayal sunk heavy like lead in his gut. "Why the hell were you so happy to see her?"

Brad twirled the bottle in his hands. "Why wouldn't I be? I haven't seen her in years."

He stared at his brother with disbelief. "Have you forgotten she could've ruined our business before we even got it off the ground?"

For a moment, surprise flickered in Brad's eyes. "Come on, she did us a favor. If it wasn't for her spreading the rumor that we were opening up a brothel and getting the town worked up about it, we wouldn't have worked so damn hard to make the workshop and caryard succeed. We wanted to prove to everyone and ourselves that we weren't just two deviants mucking around."

But what about what her leaving had done to him?

As if Brad had read his mind, he said, "She must have had a good reason for leaving."

Did his mother and brother laze around drinking tea catching up on gossip like two old ladies? His mother had said the same thing.

"It was years ago, I don't give a fuck anymore why she left."

Brad stared at him like he didn't believe him for a second but didn't utter a word.

"Why are you here?" Nick demanded for the third time and then noticed a duffle bag next to the chair Brad occupied. "Has Lexi finally come to her senses and kicked you out?" He gathered their empty bottles, threw them in the recycling, got two fresh ones, and sat back down.

Brad grinned like a man in love, and Nick wanted to wipe the sickening expression from his brother's face.

"My woman's too satisfied to kick me out. And now that she's pregnant, she wants to be satisfied more often. Hormones or something. I'm not going to complain."

Nick groaned and dropped his head in his hands. He didn't want images of his lovely sister-in-law with his idiot brother. "Too much information, bro. Seriously, how are you going to be a father when you're such a dick?" When he could see Brad was about to spout something, probably about *his* dick, he jumped in and said, "If you don't tell me why you're here, I'm going to kick your fucking arse out."

"All right, all right! I've come to drag you back to work." He'd guessed right.

"I'm not ready yet. There's too much to do here."

Brad frowned. "Percy and Kev have got the farm under control."

"Percy doesn't know how to do the books."

"Hire someone to do it." He said it as if it was so easy.

But Nick needed people here he could trust. He didn't

want just anyone sticking their noses into his father's farm, and he didn't want his mother having to worry about this stuff.

She'd been through enough.

Brad stared him down with a dubious expression.

Nick blew out a long breath. "I can't hand Dad's farm over to just anyone." He got off the stool and walked to look out the window. It continued to rain at a steady pace, and the late afternoon grew dark and ominous. "He put years of his heart into this place. The least I can do is keep it running the way he would." He heard Brad slide his chair back, and he turned to face him. Brad leaned against the counter.

"Dad never would have expected you to do this. Yeah, he loved this place, but it was *his* passion. He knew it wasn't ours." He walked over and stood beside Nick and stared out the window just like Nick had done moments ago. "Did he ever tell us he wanted us to someday take over?"

Nick shook his head.

"That's because he knew this life wasn't for us. He knew we had different plans."

"Mum loves this place too. She wouldn't want strangers running it. Who better to do it than one of her sons?"

"She wouldn't want you doing something you don't want to do either," Brad said. Nick opened his mouth to argue, but Brad cut in. "Don't you miss the company? We have a new factory opening in Singapore next month.

Normally, you would be there overseeing things. But instead you're here."

He couldn't deny there'd been a strong pull deep in his gut to get back to work. But spending time on the farm the last seven months had quietened the desire to go back. Spending time with his mother and making sure she was okay while keeping his father's business operating had been more important.

"You know what you're doing and who to send to Singapore. And I've been doing a lot from here."

Brad closed his eyes for a beat and took a deep breath. "You're missing the point. Stop playing farmer boy and get back to work. *Your* work."

Ava had called him *Old MacDonald* and now Brad called him *farmer boy*, and it pissed him off. He hadn't put his life on hold to play *pretend farmer*. This was his parents' home.

"You think I'm joking around here?" Nick paced in the small space of the kitchen. "If I wasn't running the place, who would? *You?*" He flung a hand in Brad's direction. "Your trips back home were always quick. Did you ever help Dad when you visited?"

Brad shoved his hands in his jean pockets and glared at Nick. "My visits may have been quick ones, but they were frequent, and I helped out when I could. Not that I need to explain myself." He marched toward Nick and stopped inches in front of him. His lips flattened to thin lines. "How long had it been since you'd been home before he died? Months? And the time before that? So don't point an accusing finger at me." "Fuck you." Nick curled his lip in a snarl.

Brad's shoulders sagged, and he sighed. "I'm sorry, man. Dad never expected you here all the time. He was so proud that we got off the farm and made something of ourselves."

Nick slumped on the barstool, depleted of the energy to fight. "No, you're right. I should've come home more often. I just couldn't..."

Flicking a glance in the direction of Ava's room, Brad said, "And he understood."

Nick ignored where Brad's gaze had drifted. "He understood that we needed to build our business. Nothing more." If he hadn't made it back to the farm regularly, it was because he was breaking his back getting their business off the ground. Not because of Ava and the memories that kept flooding back every time he set foot in Sunland Valley.

With a knowing expression, Brad nodded and said nothing more.

They spent the next few hours drinking beer and trading insults until Nick called it a night. He had to be up before the crack of dawn, and that was only four hours away.

He heaved himself from the couch that they'd ended up on, and pulled a blanket and pillow from a cupboard. "The couch is all yours. I can't guarantee it's comfortable."

Brad's head was tilted on the back of the cushions, his eyes heavy from too much alcohol and not enough sleep. "I thought I could sleep in your bed."

"Why the hell would you sleep with me in my bed? We're not five anymore."

A grin spread across Brad's face. "I was hoping you'd be *sleeping* in Ava's bed. *With* Ava."

Nick couldn't help but laugh. Brad and his immature brain. "Remind me again how you convinced Lexi to marry you?"

Brad kept the stupid grin on his face. "She loved my big—" A pillow slammed into Brad's face, cutting off his words.

---

## Chapter 8

---

The next morning, Ava awoke to the smell of eggs, bacon, and most importantly, coffee.

Her stomach growled at the delicious aroma. The last meal she had eaten was lunch at Maggie's.

She hadn't dared come out of her room last night to make herself something. Not with Nick and Brad having a heavy discussion. She couldn't hear what they were talking about, but their tones were grim. She didn't think Nick would have appreciated her listening.

So, she had pulled out a contract she'd brought along with her and read over her client's husband's ridiculous demands regarding their divorce settlement. No matter how many cases she handled, it still surprised her how vicious couples behaved; couples who had once declared their love in front of family, friends, and God. If Ava hadn't seen the ugliness of her parents' marriage, this surely would've swayed her off holy matrimony.

Once dressed in Maggie's borrowed clothes, Ava

ducked into the bathroom to freshen up then followed the scent of fresh coffee, passing Brad who was fast asleep on the living room couch. She found Nick in the kitchen piling a plate with eggs and bacon. His faded jeans sat low on his hips, and the army green t-shirt clung to his firm chest. Her stomach twisted, and her mouth watered. And she didn't think it had anything to do with breakfast. Damn, she had to get her body's reaction to him under control.

He glanced in her direction then turned to pick up the coffee pot. She couldn't see any of last night's heat in his eyes. Last night proved exactly what she wanted to know and more. That he wasn't indifferent. But making him prove his desire for her had caused her to sit up and take notice of long-suppressed feelings. When once, one look caused her heart to bang hard against her chest and she could never imagine being in anyone else's arms. And so, her challenge had backfired.

"Smells good. I'm starving," she said, refusing to examine it further.

He placed three eggs and strips of bacon on his plate and brought it to the breakfast counter. He pointed to the dish. "Help yourself."

Collecting a plate from the cupboard, she piled on the food. Nick raised an eyebrow.

"Don't judge. I haven't eaten since lunch yesterday."

He frowned. "Why didn't you get something to eat last night?"

"You and Brad were having girl talk. I didn't want to interrupt. I know how pissy women can get when that happens." She slid on the stool next to him, and as she did her leg brushed against his. Even through the fabric of the denim they wore, a charge of heat traveled like lightning through her veins.

Nick stilled and his eyes hooded. They sat staring at each other when Brad wandered into the kitchen. "Did someone say my name?" Yawning, he scratched the back of his head then bent down and kissed Ava's cheek. "Morning, sweetheart. Thought you'd be long gone by now. The rain stopped."

How did she not notice? She scampered to the window and peered outside. Sure enough, no more rain. Not only that, the sky was clear of dark clouds and was now a brilliant blue. Like the rain-soaked sky from the past two days had never existed.

She smiled and sat back down and attacked breakfast with enthusiasm. "I'll collect my stuff and we can go in ten minutes."

Nick shook his head. "Sorry, not going to happen."

She paused with a fork full of bacon suspended in mid-air. "Why the hell not?"

She didn't want to spend another minute more than she had to closed up with Nick.

"The road is still flooded." He picked up his plate, rinsed it, and placed it in the dishwasher.

"How do you know? The rain's stopped."

"Unlike the two of you, I've been up for hours. I've checked." He gave Brad a disgusted look, but he only smiled back and threw a piece of bacon in his mouth. "We've had a lot of rain, it needs time to go somewhere."

"But now that the rain's stopped you can get me back home using the highway." She was impatient to leave. Being alone with Nick had proved too hazardous. And Bella needed her, so the sooner she sorted that out, the sooner she could go home to Brimland Point and back to her own life.

"I'll have a lot to do now that the weather's cleared. The earliest I can do it is this afternoon."

"This afternoon!" Ava sighed and slumped her shoulders. Stay a few more hours or call her father to pick her up? She had no desire to see the man at all, and she certainly didn't want to be stuck in a car with him, because then she might have to actually talk to him. It looked like she was staying.

Brad sat next to her. "Don't look so disappointed. It's not every day you're lucky enough to spend the morning with two sexy Williams men." He winked at her, and she rolled her eyes but laughed at his comical expression.

"So, you're planning on helping with the cows today?" Nick asked Brad.

"Ahh, as much as I'd love to, I promised Mum I'd help her frame some photos."

Nick snorted. "Anything to get out of a little hard work."

"Have you seen how many photos she wants me to frame? She's selling bucket loads."

That reminded Ava to talk to Lauren about selling some in her gift shop. She was sure Lauren would love them. She needed to take photos and send them to her friend before she left Sunland Valley.

"When did you become such a pussy?" Nick gave Brad a disgusted look.

"Not a pussy, little bro." He tapped the side of his head with his index finger. "Smart." He shoved back from the counter and strolled into the living room. Ava assumed to get ready to go help Maggie.

"I guess farming life isn't for everyone," she said to fill the awkward silence that had fallen over the kitchen once Brad left.

"Brad never liked it much. Always had an excuse for getting out of work."

The tension from last night easing, she smiled. She remembered. Nick had always been the one to do everything he could to help out in his spare time. Brad would be nowhere to be seen. That was how she had spent a lot of her time with Nick. Riding along in his truck, checking on cows and fences and anything that needed to be done. And discovering secret hiding places where they couldn't keep their hands off each other.

She jerked herself out of her nostalgia and rose to put her plate in the dishwasher. Then made to leave the kitchen to let Nick do whatever he had planned for the day.

"Feel like going for a drive around the farm?" he asked.

His back was turned away from her while he cleared the dishes, so she couldn't see his expression. Was he being serious?

"Now that the sun's out I thought you might like to see the place again after all these years."

He *was* serious. He was really offering to take her out with him.

She froze for a beat. He'd been doing everything he could to stay away from her, and after last night, she thought he'd be scurrying away. If she were smart, she should be running too, but she glanced out the window. The day was too beautiful to stay indoors, and she would love to see the farm after being away so long.

"Give me a sec to put on my shoes."

"I'll wait for you outside."

Nick threw the gear he needed for the day in the tray of the truck and whistled for Molly to jump in. He secured her safely and scratched her behind the ears, and her tongue rolled out in pure bliss. "Why can't all women be as uncomplicated as you, Molly?" Molly nuzzled her face on Nick's chest.

What was he thinking asking Ava to come for a drive? One minute he couldn't stand being in the same room, and the next, the words spewed out of his big mouth, sounding eager to spend the day with her. Tightness squeezed his heart. Even with the ghosts of the past playing with his mind, he had a hard time staying away. And what was even more surprising, she'd agreed to come along.

She made her way over to the truck wearing the too-big jeans and joggers his mother had given her and one of his jumpers. There was nothing sexy about the clothes, but she'd be dropdead gorgeous in anything.

"I'm looking more like a farm girl each day, don't you think?" Placing her hand on her hip, she struck a pose.

A farm girl was not the term he'd use, and he stared at her longer than the situation required. She dropped the playful stance, stared back, and stepped closer. She must've read the hunger in his eyes, because her chest rose and fell at a rapid pace and she glanced at his mouth.

Molly barked, impatient to get going or wanting attention, and the moment was broken.

Nick stepped away and scratched Molly behind the ear. "Okay, girl, let's go." He jumped in the truck and Ava followed.

The next hour was spent checking on fences, and Nick listened to Ava's commentary on everything she remembered and all the things that had been added since she'd been gone. Would she be remembering what they'd gotten up to in some of those secluded places too? If she did, she said nothing.

How many times had he driven along these roads imagining Ava by his side when he finally made it off the farm and had built a bigger and better life? He'd always pictured a future together. But they'd been kids. Even if she hadn't left, it probably never would've worked. Hell, who knew if it would have lasted much longer than that summer. What once felt like a stab to the chest now only stung a little. It had only taken ten years.

"Nick, stop!"

He had already seen what had made her yell and was

braking. At the dam, a calf, chest deep in mud, was struggling to free itself. Its mother stood by its side, mooing in distress.

He vaulted out of the truck, pulled out rope, and ran to it. The calf, tired from struggling, laid its head in the mud. It'd probably been stuck for a while and was starting to weaken.

Heaving the calf's head from the mud, Nick gave it a reassuring pat. "Hang in there, mate. I'll get you out."

He wrapped the rope around its neck and turned to find Ava knee-deep in mud next to him, concern for the animal etched on her face.

"What can I do to help?"

"I need you to back the truck up as close as you can without hitting the mud. I'll tie the end of the rope to the towbar."

She nodded, got back in the truck, and reversed it. Nick held up his hand, indicating when to stop. He tied the rope to the towbar as she rushed back and took his spot next to the calf, cooing in the animal's ear like she was settling a baby.

Once the rope was secure he said, "Okay, I need you to drive out slowly."

As the truck shifted forward, he began lifting and pulling the distressed animal. After a few stops and starts, trying to haul a nearly two hundred kilo calf from the mud, they finally had it free and with its mother. Nick slapped them both on the rump to shoo them away from the soggy dam.

Ava bounded from the truck, ran to Nick, and threw

her arms around him. "We did it!" Then she stiffened, pulled away, and stepped back. She grimaced at his clothes then at her own and laughed. "I don't think Maggie's going to want this back." She wrinkled her nose. "I don't think it's only mud."

He untied the rope and winded it up to distract himself. Her exuberance reminded him of when they were younger.

"I know somewhere we can clean up." He threw the rope in the tray.

After getting back in the truck, they drove a few minutes to a cluster of eucalyptus trees, parked the car, and got out. It was a place they'd went to often, and sure enough, excitement lit her dirty face when she realized where they were going. They'd spent hours at this waterhole, swimming, skinny-dipping, and having way too much fun.

The track there was now overgrown with infrequent use. The last time he'd trekked this path was with Ava. It took them twenty minutes to hike through the bush to get to the pool of water nestled under the cliffs. The sound of the waterfall, which was usually a slow trickle, was now a hard rush after the heavy rain.

"This place is still so beautiful," Ava said in awe as they both stared out over the boulders of rocks that formed the pool surrounded by gumtrees. The waterfall crashed down, causing choppy ripples on the surface.

She tugged off her shoes, rolled up the bottom of her jeans, and climbed up onto the boulders until she found a spot she could dangle her feet into the water. She reached in and rinsed off the mud on her arms and tried to wipe some off her jeans.

Molly sniffed around until she found the tree she wanted to lie under and fell fast asleep.

With mud caked all over him, Nick joined Ava and began to wash as much off as he could. She leaned back on her hands, tilted her face to the sun, closed her eyes, and sighed. Like she was releasing the weight of the world.

"We don't have places like this back home," she said as she kicked her feet in the water.

He noticed that she referred to where she was living now as home and not the place where she grew up.

"We have beautiful beaches, which I don't go to often enough, but there's something about being in the middle of nature with no one around. The colors, the sounds… it's so peaceful. Do you know what I mean?"

She twirled around and gave him a smile that smacked him right in the chest. She was beautiful, he couldn't deny it, and when she smiled like that, her whole face lit up and he couldn't breathe for a moment. Warmth and something tingly spread through his veins.

"Yeah, it's spectacular out here." His voice was gruff. It wasn't the scenery he was talking about.

She laid back on the rock, stretched her arms over her head, and made a little groaning sound. A burst of fire shot straight to his groin. She was killing him, and if she kept looking so damn sexy, he was going to do something stupid again.

He jumped up, pulled his t-shirt over his head, and tossed it on the rock.

Her eyes widened. "What are you doing?"

"I need to get the mud off," he lied. He needed to take care of the problem throbbing in his jeans, and there were only two ways to deal with that. One involved Ava and the other was a dunk in the cold water. He chose the latter.

"You can't be serious about going for a swim in that!" She sat up and pointed at the water. "It's so murky after all the rain."

"Where's your sense of adventure? Years ago, you would've been the first one in."

"I don't have a death wish anymore." She grimaced.

"Or you've gotten old," he teased.

Her eyes narrowed, but he didn't wait for her reply. He had more pressing issues to deal with. Taking a deep breath, he jumped into the water.

When he surfaced, he shook his head and droplets flew from his hair. Ava stood on the rocks, hands on hips, glaring at him. Even with her lethal expression and the blast of cold water, it did nothing to ease his discomfort.

"Just because I don't want to hurdle myself into dangerous, murky water doesn't make me old. I've obviously acquired a lot more common sense over the years than you."

"Okay."

She crossed her arms over her chest. "I'm intelligent enough to know not to jump in there."

"Whatever you say."

"You don't believe me."

He shrugged as he treaded water. "Sure I do."

It wasn't hard to see that she had recognized the sarcasm. She blew out a frustrated breath and glanced suspiciously at the water. After what appeared to be her battling an argument in her mind, she squared her shoulders and stared at him with a challenging expression.

Without breaking eye contact, she pulled the jumper over her head and tossed it on top of his t-shirt. Then she peeled off her jeans, and they too got tossed aside, leaving her in nothing but a tiny, lacy, pink bra and matching undies.

Nick's heart thumped hard in his ribcage, and the organ he'd been trying to contain had now grown double in size and double the trouble.

She raised a dark eyebrow, and her lips twitched. Yeah, she knew exactly how to use her body to bring a man to his knees, or in his case, drown. Then she jumped into the turbulent water.

## Chapter 9

The chilly water sluiced over Ava's heated skin, doing little to reduce the sudden rush of heat that had blasted through her body when Nick took off his shirt. The ropy muscles of his arms had rippled as he'd pulled the t-shirt over his head. Then her eyes had trailed to an impressive chest and abs. A sprinkling of dark hair traveled down along his corrugated stomach and disappeared behind the waistband of his jeans. The boy had grown nicely into a man. She'd had to stop herself from reaching out and trailing her hand along his body.

It had been two months since she'd had a man in her life, or more to the point, had sex. *A man in her life* implied a relationship, and that's what Ava avoided. Sex, yes. Relationships, no. Her father had taught her early on how poisoning they could be. And she dealt with more divorces at her law firm than she could count. At first when she'd lost interest in sex she'd thought something might be physically wrong and went to see the doctor. After a physical that showed no signs of anything sinister, the doctor's diagnosis was overwork and stress.

If she was being honest with herself, picking up a random guy had lost its appeal, but that didn't mean she wanted to go down the relationship route. Now, after spending the past two days with Nick, kissing him and seeing his hotter than hell body, all her good parts had woken up. She wanted to raise her hands to the sky and yell *halleluiah, praise the Lord, I am cured!*

But why did Nick have to be the cure? Why not the cute guy with the dimples who tried picking her up at Dexter's? He could have been the one. But when his hands wandered to places that normally buzzed with excitement, it had only creeped her out. Now Nick had gotten those places buzzing again and in the most delicious way.

As she swam toward Nick, heat sparked from his eyes, and he watched her like he wanted to take a bite. She quivered, imagining the body parts she'd love for him to sink his teeth into.

As much as she craved for him to feast on all the places that tingled with goodness, she couldn't go there. If he kissed her again like he did last night, and with her libido back in action, she knew how this story would end. They'd end up naked, having sex, and as soon as she was back on the road, they'd go their separate ways.

But wasn't that exactly how she liked things? No attachments? A tightness clutched at her chest. The ache wasn't something she was used to. Why didn't *no-strings sex* seem right with Nick? Maybe the uneasiness had something to do with the history they shared.

"Stop looking at me with those come-sex-me-up eyes," she ordered. She schooled her face so she didn't stare back at him with the same lusty expression. Although her sex-starved body wanted exactly what his eyes suggested, her mind was trying to overrule.

He shifted closer, keeping buoyant in the rough water. Her arms and legs were already starting to tire, and she hadn't been in the water as long as he had. She'd either have to wrap her legs around Nick to keep afloat or head back to shore. Using him as a floatation device did sound appealing, but it would mean trouble.

"I think you like it when I look at you with come-sex-me-up eyes." His voice was low and sexy. For a man who only a day ago couldn't move far enough away, he was fast approaching. A witty comeback clogged in her throat.

He treaded in closer, bopping in the water so close that their chests almost touched. God, why did guys look so hot wet? Him looking like that made it so much harder to think. It was time to make up her mind. Was she going to sink or swim?

His eyes hooded as he leaned closer, their lips only a hair's breadth away. If they touched, it would surely make her sink. So she lifted her arm and splashed water in his face.

"What the fuck!" he spluttered.

Now it was time to swim. Ava didn't wait around. She went full free-style stroke mode toward the rocks. Only to be pulled up by her left ankle and dragged back.

She managed a gurgled squeal and swallowed a mouthful of water just before her head got thrust under the surface. When she resurfaced, coughing and spluttering, she pushed clumps of hair from her eyes and glared at Nick's laughing face.

"What's the matter, Avi-baby, can't take a bit of payback?" He called her Avi-baby again, but this time he didn't look annoyed about the slipped nickname.

"I only splashed a tiny bit of water at you. You could've drowned me."

His grin grew wider. "You're exaggerating." Another wave of water flew in his face.

She dodged his outstretched arms and swam as fast as she could to safety, but once again, a firm hand wrapped around her ankle and reeled her in like a fish. This time pulling her to him so her back pressed up against his chest. He wrapped his arms around her waist, supporting her.

He must have found a boulder to stand on because he was steady.

Not like her trembling heart—there was nothing steady about it.

"Ava," he whispered in a deep, husky voice.

Wet, hot lips at the nape of her neck sent her body into a shivering mess, and her head dropped back to rest on his shoulder. She couldn't stop him if she'd tried.

"You're driving me crazy. I don't know if I want to strangle you or screw you," he said as his hands skimmed her stomach.

Ava pulled in a sharp breath.

His hands continued to glide up her torso until they paused under her heaving breasts. She arched her back, giving him permission to handle them. But instead of taking them like she desperately wanted him to, he slid his hands to her back and gave her a gentle shove toward the shore.

The rebuff shocked her more than diving into the frigid water. He'd pushed her away just when her body was responding and craving his touch. How dare he turn her on and off like a light switch then leave her wanting more. No man had ever rejected her, and he'd done it twice! Even though last night was a test, it had gone way beyond a challenge and he'd been the one to put a stop to it. She always got what she wanted, and at the moment, even though her mind protested, her body was seeking one hot, sexy farmer boy.

Rising out of the waterhole, she stood, hands on hips, glaring down at Nick who was now doing laps in the pool. It was evident he'd wanted her too; it had pressed firmly against her arse. While she had no release for her frustrations, he was swimming like an Olympic swimmer to get rid of his.

Feeling drained, she heaved a heavy sigh, dropped onto a boulder flat enough to lie on, and soaked up the sun to dry while she waited for Nick to finish. A good time later, a splashing sound and footsteps on the rocks announced his exit from the water. She grinned with satisfaction. That was a long time to get himself under control. It served the jerk right.

He sucked in a breath and growled, "Fuck me." And

her grin exploded into a huge, teethbaring smile. She hadn't bothered dressing, and she lay on the boulder, knowing exactly how she looked in her Victoria's Secret underwear.

"Need to do a few more laps?" she said sweetly as she raised onto her elbows. Then she scrambled to her feet and rushed to Nick's side. "You're bleeding." A trickle of blood made a trail down his bristly cheek.

He swiped at the blood with the back of his hand, not taking his heavy-lidded eyes off her. "Why aren't you dressed?"

"I wanted to dry." And make him suffer for turning her into a quivering mess.

More blood sprang from a small cut, and she reached out to stroke his cheek.

Nick clutched her wrist, his eyes darkening to a stormy blue. "Touch me and you're gonna find yourself lying on that rock again, touching more than my face."

Her insides did a shimmy and a shake at the prospect, but she'd regained control of her body and knew to leave well enough alone. "But the blood—"

"It's nothing. A branch pricked me. Let's go." He spun on his heel, picked up his shirt, and whistled for Molly to follow him. "I'll wait for you at the truck."

The tension that had begun to slip between them during the day, sprung back up in full force. For a few hours they'd forgotten the resentment they'd had for one another and enjoyed each other's company like they were friends. But they weren't friends. She wasn't sure they could ever be again.

Before leaving, she took one last look at the water-hole. The choppy, murky water didn't detract from the beauty of the place. She never thought she'd be back here to see it again, and sadly, this would be the last time. Once she got off the farm and sorted out why Bella needed her, she'd be back at Brimland Point and getting back to her life. One that didn't include a moody, but sexy, farmer boy.

Collecting her clothes, she quickly dressed and headed in the direction of where they'd parked. Luckily for him, she knew the track back, otherwise, she would have ripped into him for leaving her in the middle of nowhere.

When she reached him, he was securing Molly into the tray.

"Why so hot and cold?" The words left her mouth before she had time to stop them. That was so unlike her, especially with her career. She needed to gather information, look at things a hundred different ways. Not just blurt out whatever wanted to come out of her mouth. But the words were out now, and she couldn't take them back. May as well see what the attitude was about.

He flicked a brief glance over his shoulder and patted Molly's head. "Am I supposed to know what you're talking about?"

"Don't play dumb." She gritted her teeth. "One minute you're hot and heavy, looking at me like I'm your next meal, and the next you're blowing more cold air than the Antarctic."

He swiveled and met her gaze. "Did you want me to screw you back there? Because we were two seconds away from that happening, and believe me, as good as it would have been, it wouldn't have been worth it." He slammed the tailgate closed.

Fury boiled in her stomach. "You're an arsehole."

He slumped his shoulders and shook his head like he'd lost the urge to fight. "We've gone down that road before and look how that turned out."

*And who's fault was that?* she wanted to yell. If he hadn't betrayed her, things could've been different. But would they have lasted? They'd had their own dreams and ambitions. Hers was taking her out of Sunland Valley. She thought Nick would have been long gone by now too.

She leaned her butt on the side of the truck, watching Nick. She could tell by the raised eyebrow he was waiting for her to disagree. Their relationship hadn't ended well, she couldn't deny it.

"We were young. What did we know about relationships?"

He ran his fingers through his wet hair. "Nothing."

"And we're both still clueless." She laughed to try to make light of it, but it sounded flat.

He smirked, but no warmth reached his eyes. "Yeah, we are."

Chapter 10

$\mathcal{N}$ick dropped Ava back at the house so she could clean up before she left. He had work he needed to finish, and she was too much of a distraction. When he found Percy filling his truck with hay, the old farmer had everything under control.

"What about the troughs?" Nick asked. "Had to rescue a calf stuck in mud from the south dam trying to get to the water. I don't want the cows near the dams until it dries up."

"Taken care of. Kev and a couple of the farmhands have moved them to the top paddock and secured them in. I'll be taking this hay up to them."

"The hay bales are looking low. I'll need to order more."

Percy shook his head. "On their way."

With his hands on hips, Nick glanced around, trying to look for something that needed to be done.

"Nick, mate, go home. Everything is handled."

By *home*, Nick knew Percy meant Sydney. But he couldn't abandon the farm. It needed to be run by a Williams. His father had put too many years into this place for it to be operated by anyone other than family. Brad might believe their father wanted them to pursue their own dreams, but deep down, Nick knew it would have made him happy if one of his sons took over.

What would happen with his business if he stayed? With a factory opening in Singapore and more caryards opening around the county, business had never been stronger. How could Brad run the corporation without him? They had executives and a bunch of staff to help do the job, but they were responsible for running the company. Nick and Brad oversaw everything.

And now Nick had left Brad to do things himself with a pregnant wife to look after. Nick could do a lot away from the office, but it wasn't the same as being amongst it all. He should be in Singapore overseeing the work. Producing their own cars had been a dream come true. They were going to give other car companies a run for their money. Their sleek new vehicles would be on a lot of people's wish list.

But he knew he couldn't do both, something had to give. For now, until he worked something out, he would do what needed to be done on the farm.

Later that afternoon, after giving Percy a hand even though he insisted he had everything covered, he checked on Ava's car and the road into town. He went to the house and found Ava back in his t-shirt, curled up and sleeping on the couch. Even in her sleep she looked sexy as hell, and he couldn't help but let his eyes wander over her exposed legs. Legs that he'd dreamed of being wrapped around him. His stomach clenched at the thought.

Not wanting to wake her, he quickly showered and went into the kitchen to prepare dinner. He pulled out two T-bone steaks from the freezer, put them in the microwave to defrost, and grabbed a premade bag of salad from the fridge.

As he was taking the steaks from the microwave, Ava walked into the kitchen. She yawned and stretched her arms above her head, hiking the hem of her t-shirt dangerously close to exposing whatever color panties she'd changed into. And dammit he wanted to know.

"Sorry, I didn't mean to wake you," he said, his voice gruff, as he carried the steaks outside to the barbeque and away from the woman who kept giving him a mega hard-on.

Unfortunately, she followed and leaned against the veranda railing, watching him cook.

"I thought you'd like to eat before I take you home," he said as he threw the steaks on the grill.

Her eyebrows lifted, but she didn't demand to be taken back straight away.

He seasoned the meat, and it sizzled and popped on the heat. "I have some bad news for you."

She narrowed her eyes. "The rain's stopped, I can leave. How can there be bad news?"

"Your car's missing all four tires."

"What?" she yelled, shoving away from the railing.

"Your car's missing all four—"

"I heard you the first time!"

Nick couldn't help but snigger.

"Oh, you think this is funny, do you?"

He wiped the smile off his face, but his lips still twitched. "Not at all."

"I thought you've been checking my car?" she said with an accusatory tone.

"I have. They were on yesterday."

She paced the small veranda, and Nick's gaze dropped to her toned, tanned legs. Once again he imagined how they'd feel wrapped around him as he pressed her up against the wall… He shook his head, trying to dislodge the image.

Then, with her hands on her hips, she stopped in front of him, glaring. "Are you listening?"

No, his brain had shut off and another organ had been doing the thinking. God, this woman was driving him insane. The sooner she left, the better off he'd be. Or the sooner they screwed, he'd feel even better. And the longer she stayed, the more tempting it was, and damn the consequences.

"Who would want to steal Mercedes tires? It's not like many are driven around here."

"It was most likely a couple of kids. They'll sell them."

"Kids? What kind of delinquents are running around Sunland Valley now?" She huffed.

Nick laughed. "They've always been here. Weren't *we* delinquents once?" He flipped the steaks and leaned back on the veranda railing. "How many times did we break into Sunland Valley High, steal all the toilet paper, and TP the classrooms?"

Ava smirked.

"Or when we used to steal the bike tires from Principal Mooney's bike and roll them down his driveway," he said.

Averting her gaze, she bit her lip to stop from laughing but couldn't hold it back. "God, we were bad. How did we never get caught? And you should have known better, you were older. What a bad influence you were."

Laughing, Nick lifted the steaks from the grill, placed them on two plates, and carried them to the kitchen. Ava followed.

"Never got caught?" They sat at the dining table, and he poured them some wine. "Man, I got busted so many times. I was lucky my old man was friends with Sergeant Finlay or I would have been in deep shit."

Ava blinked with surprise. "But I never got in trouble?"

"That's because whenever the cops came knocking on my parents' door, asking to see me, I told them I was the only one involved."

"I didn't know you did that." She smiled then shuddered with a laugh. "My father would've killed me."

"I copped an ear bashing from my parents. Then they

had me shoveling cow shit for the next week. And now you're defending those delinquents."

"You know I'm a lawyer?"

"It was all you ever wanted to be. I just assumed." He'd looked her up a time or two— only out of curiosity —but he'd keep that to himself.

"I'm surprised you remembered. My specialty… divorce." She raised her glass like a toast.

"You sound like you're happy about people getting divorced."

"Not at all," she said. "People shouldn't marry at all, and if they're stupid enough to do so, they should see me first. I'll set them up with a perfect pre-nup no one can dispute."

Nick sat back in his chair and took a big swallow of wine. "You don't believe a marriage can last?"

"Besides your parents, I've never seen it happen. Or rather, I've never seen a happy one last."

"So cynical."

She twirled the stem of her glass between her fingers. "Have you been married?" He nodded.

For a beat, her eyebrows rose, then she dropped her gaze to her glass. "Unless you're a cheating arsehole, I'm assuming you're divorced. And I bet it ended badly." When he didn't answer, she took his silence as agreement.

"You're not the only one. It happens all the time. If you ever have the crazy notion to do it again, come and see me."

He wouldn't be heading down that road anytime

soon, but he didn't discard marriage altogether. His marriage may have been a disaster, and he'd take full responsibility for his part, but he'd seen plenty of happy ones.

"Marriages aren't all bad. Brad's happily married, and my parents were too."

Ava examined his face, and when she must've decided he was telling the truth, she said, "You're right. On a rare occasion, it can happen. I'd still strongly advise a pre-nup."

He couldn't disagree with her there. If he hadn't had one when he'd married Kate, he would've lost a shitload of money and property. Kate still became a wealthy woman after the settlement, but she quickly blew it away.

"How long where you married?" Ava asked.

"Two years."

She topped their wine glasses. "What happened?"

Straight to the point. Ava never did tiptoe around things. "I made the mistake of marrying for lust rather than love. She'd been in love. It didn't take her long to realize her feelings weren't reciprocated." After Ava, his heart couldn't open up to love again.

She made a tsking sound and shook her head. "That must've gotten ugly."

He laughed without humor. "To put it lightly."

"How long did it take her to realize you weren't in love?"

If they were going to talk about this, he needed something stronger than wine. He stood and went into the kitchen to fetch a bottle of Jack. When he got back to the table Ava's brow rose like she was still waiting for an answer. Or was surprised he needed extra-strength liquid to continue the conversation.

He poured the whiskey into two fresh glasses, handed one to her, and tossed his back. "I think Kate always knew deep down it wasn't love-hearts and roses. Maybe she hoped in time it would change. I hoped so too." He shrugged then poured more whiskey and tossed it back again while Ava still sipped on her first. "I tried to give her what she needed…"

"You can't force what's not there," she finished for him.

He nodded. "I never should have married her in the first place."

"We all make mistakes. Where is she now?"

This was the toughest part about their marriage. If he'd loved her like she'd needed, maybe she wouldn't have spiraled out of control. "The Burrows."

Ava's eyes widened. "The rehabilitation clinic?"

"Yes."

"Drugs or alcohol?"

"Drugs."

She sat back in her chair and blew out a long breath. "That's intense. How long has she been there?"

Nick rubbed the back of his neck. "Six months next week."

Ava whistled. "She must be dealing with some bad demons to be in there so long." Her eyes narrowed as she stared at him. "And you feel responsible." She said it like she could read his thoughts, because it was a statement not a question.

He couldn't help but feel responsible.

Leaning forward, she slid her hand on the top of the table toward Nick's, and then, as if realizing what she was doing, pulled back. "Unless you held her down and pumped the drugs into her, it's not your fault."

"After we got married I found out that she'd been using drugs for years. I should've known how bad she'd gotten, tried harder to make our marriage work. Instead, I spent most of my time at work, ignoring what was happening at home."

"It was *her* choice to deal with it that way. It's not *your* fault."

The tight feeling in his gut when he thought of Kate loosened slightly at hearing Ava acknowledge he wasn't to blame for his ex-wife's addiction. He smiled his gratitude.

"What made you decide to end the marriage?"

This was the part that had been seared into his brain. He wanted to reach in and tear the memory out and never relive it again. "I got home one night and she'd thrown a party. I went looking for her and found her in our bedroom."

"Uh-oh," she said like she knew what was coming, but she really had no idea.

"She was on our bed…sniffing blow off some fat, old, rich guy's dick." Ava's mouth dropped open.

"I later found out that her advertising business had gone broke and she had no money. And she didn't want to ask me for more because she knew I'd ask questions, so she found some rich bastard to fund her addiction."

"Oh my God!" Ava slumped back on the chair. "Gives a whole new meaning to the term *blow job*, doesn't it?" Her lips twitched, and she bit her bottom lip to stop herself from smiling.

Scrubbing his face with his hands, Nick tried to hide his own smile. It definitely hadn't been funny at the time. It had made his balls shrink so far into his body he was worried he'd never see them again. At the sound of Ava's laugh his shoulders shook and he couldn't help but join in.

"I haven't been able to look at fat, rich guys the same way again." Their laughter grew louder.

When they sobered up, Ava slid her hand across the table and this time didn't pull back.

She placed it on top of his and squeezed. "She's in the best place to get help."

"Yeah, I know." He'd do whatever it took to get her better. And based on the monthly reports the clinic was sending him, she was doing well and would be ready to be discharged in a couple of weeks.

They took their dirty dishes into the kitchen and loaded the dishwasher. It had grown dark and he was supposed to have driven Ava into town.

"I've had a few drinks, I can't take you home. Is there someone you can call to come and pick you up?" It surprised him that Ava hadn't already demanded to be taken into town. All she'd wanted to do was get off the farm.

She glanced out the window, tugging at her bottom lip in thought, not looking impatient to leave. "Do you mind if I stay another night? It's late." He must have had a surprised expression on his face, because she quickly added, "I don't want to bother anyone at this hour, and I'd like to see Maggie before I go."

"Sure."

They stared at each other for a beat. Tonight, he'd opened up about Kate like he'd never done before. Ava was always a good listener and could make light of things to ease the tension.

The temptation to haul her into his arms was strong. He itched to touch her, mold her body against his and claim her lips. But he had to resist the urge. If he went there with her, could he drag himself back out?

"Well, I'll see you in the morning," he said, then shuffled toward his bedroom.

"Good night," she called after him.

"Night," he answered without turning back.

---

Ava sat in the living room, not yet ready for bed, her mind racing with the crazy couple of days she'd had. Never in a million years did she think she'd be alone with Nick in this house again. During the last two days, they'd gone from hating one another to wanting to crawl over each other to… What were they now? After he'd opened up about his ex-wife could they be friends? He didn't look at her like he wanted to be friends, and with the way her skin flushed hot, she didn't think she could put him in the friend zone either.

Her mobile rang, stopping her from analyzing her reaction to him too closely. It didn't matter anyway; she'd be gone in the morning. Padding on bare feet to where she'd left her phone on the coffee table, she picked it up to see Jade's smiling face. Ava smiled back at the photo.

God, she missed her friend. She hadn't spoken to the girls since leaving Brimland Point.

She swiped the screen to accept Jade's Facetime call. Her pretty face and big smile filled the screen. She'd tied her red, curly hair up in a messy bun and springs of curls framed her face. "Ava, I've missed you!"

Ava laughed. "Missed you too, honey."

"How did things go with Isabella?" Jade asked.

"It hasn't." Ava got herself comfortable on the couch and told her about the storm.

"Who's this friend you're staying with?"

Before she could come up with a fabricated friend—because she'd never told the girls about Nick and didn't want to explain him to her now—Jade's eyes widened, and she whispered, "Who is that?"

Ava's stomach dropped. There could only be one person standing behind her.

Tilting her head to look at Nick over her shoulder, her breath caught in her throat. He stood at his bedroom doorway only wearing black boxer briefs that clung tightly around an impressive package, scratching his hard, tanned chest. Bed hair made him look hotter than hell, and she wanted to run her fingers through the messy locks.

"Sorry, I didn't mean to interrupt." He jerked a finger toward the kitchen. "Need a glass of water."

"Ava!" Jade's voice was high-pitched. Ava swung back to look at Jade. "Aren't you going to introduce me to your *friend?*"

No, she didn't want to introduce Jade to Nick, because she couldn't trust what might came out of Jade's mouth. But because she couldn't say that without Nick overhearing, she sighed and called him, stopping him before he reached the kitchen. "Come and say hi to my friend Jade."

Walking back, he stood behind Ava and bent down to get in line with the camera on the phone. Their faces almost pressed together, and his warm breath fanned along her neck. Ava shivered.

"This is my friend Nick. Nick, this is Jade."

"Hi, Jade." Nick waved.

Jade gave a little finger-wiggle wave back. "Nice meeting you, Nick. Are you and Ava having a lovely time being stranded on the farm together?"

Ava threw Jade a warning glare, but Nick chuckled low and deep. Her heart accelerated. If she moved a little closer and tilted her head just right, his mouth could… God, she was Facetiming Jade and picturing making out with Nick. What was wrong with her?

"It's been interesting getting reacquainted," he said.

"Oh, reacquainted? So, how long have you known each other?" Jade raised an eyebrow, giving Ava an accusatory look.

"About ten years," he answered.

"Ten years!" This time Jade's eyebrows propelled into her hairline, and her mouth dropped open.

The only male friends Ava told the girls about were the ones that lasted one night or two. It wasn't surprising Jade found this bit of information shocking. Then she pinned Ava with a questioning stare, like she was one of her kindergarten students needing to explain themselves to get out of trouble.

Either Nick sensed something between Ava and Jade or he just wasn't into any more chitchat, because he chose that moment to take off. "I'll leave you two alone. Nice meeting you, Jade."

Jade's blue eyes sparkled with excitement as she beamed back at him. "Bye, Nick."

Placing a finger on her lips, Ava stopped Jade from blubbering anything until he got his water and went back into the bedroom.

"What the hell have you been hiding from us?" Jade burst out as soon as he closed the door.

"Shush."

Ava glanced over her shoulder to check that he was really gone. But just to make sure he didn't overhear them, she went into the kitchen. Knowing Jade and the questions she no doubt would fire at her, she could be there for a while, so she decided to make hot chocolate. Propping the phone against a sugar canister, she maneuvered around the kitchen, gathering ingredients.

"Will you stop moving around and explain why you've never mentioned Mr. Hotness before? And the *real* reason you're staying with him."

Scooping cocoa powder and sugar into a small pot of milk, she turned on the stove. "The *real* reason why I'm staying here is exactly what I told you earlier. I got stranded in a storm." She picked up a spoon and whisked the milk to help dissolve the sugar.

"No, you don't stop there, missy. I want to know how you've been friends for ten years and you've never told us about him before."

Ava shifted uncomfortably. How much should she tell Jade? Not because she didn't trust her—she could tell her anything—but because she didn't know how she would feel dragging it back up again.

Probably doubting she was going to answer, Jade said, "If he hadn't told me you've been friends for years, I would've thought he was only a hook-up, but I'm sensing something more than that. But I know you don't take things further. So I'm confused."

Ava had explained to the girls what kind of marriage her parents had and how she never wanted to go down that path. They couldn't understand the extreme measurements she went to in order to avoid relationships, but they respected her decision.

"Nick and I dated when I lived in Sunland Valley. Not for long, around three months." And in such a short time she'd forgotten everything she hated about her parents' relationship and fell hard for Nick. It had been the best summer of her life.

"What happened?" Jade prompted.

"I moved to Brimland Point, and we lost contact." She lifted the pot off the stove and poured the steaming milk into a *Farmers Do It Better* mug. That she could believe. One hot farmer who was in his room had exceptional skills.

Jade shook her head, causing curls to spring from the bun. "I can tell there's definitely more to this story."

Ava picked up the phone and mug and sat at the breakfast counter. "You can, can you?"

She had to laugh. "You're so nosy."

"Yes, I know. Now fill me in. I have all night." She sighed. "There's no hot guy warming up my bed tonight." Then her eyes lit up. "Am I keeping you from Mr. Hotness? Of course I am.

We can talk tomorrow."

"No… No, you're not. It's not what you're thinking."

"Why the hell not? Have you seen what he looks like? And that body… Holy moley, Ava, I could lick it. I can't because I'm here and he's there, and I wouldn't because… well, he's yours. Dammit, why do you and Lauren get all the hot ones?"

Ava laughed. She didn't blame Jade's reaction, the thought had crossed her mind once or twice, or a hundred times, too. "He is good to look at," she admitted.

"So why haven't you done anything about it? You would never let someone like him go to waste."

Of course that's what Jade would think. Because Ava was so against relationships, she'd used her active sex drive to have brief encounters. What used to be fun and exciting somehow now made her feel heartless and empty. How different was she really from her father? He couldn't keep it in his pants, and apparently neither could she. She was more like him than she wanted to believe. The only difference was she wasn't married and hurting someone. But how many times had she seen concern on Jade and Lauren's faces when she left a club with a random stranger?

"Ava, are you okay?" Jade's voice broke through her musings.

She wrapped her hands around her warm mug as if trying to draw the heat into her cold body. "Sorry, my mind wandered off."

"It was more than a summer fling, wasn't it?" she gently prodded.

Ava nodded as she took a sip of the hot chocolate and gathered her thoughts. "As I said, we dated for three months. We were inseparable. Every spare minute we had was spent together, getting up to crazy things, or making out." She smiled at the memory. "I finally thought I could see past my parents' shitty relationship and believe in love." She shrugged the heaviness from her shoulders.

"He didn't love you back?" Jade asked.

Ava shook her head. "No. My father didn't like Nick and offered him a large sum of money to stay away from me."

Jade gasped and put a hand over her mouth. "Tell me he didn't take it."

Ava swallowed hard, the bitter taste of betrayal rising in her throat. "Dad said he didn't think twice about taking the money."

"Oh, Ava."

She waved a hand to dismiss Jade's sympathy. "It's

history. We've moved on." Although there had been plenty of moments when they'd snapped each other's heads off, now they were precariously starting to get along.

"It must be hard staying there with all that history hanging over your heads." Ava finished her drink and slid the mug onto the kitchen counter. "It was at first." "At first…" Jade's eyes narrowed with suspicion.

She rolled her eyes. "We've gotten a little more comfortable around each other."

"So you *are* sleeping together?"

"No, but we've…made out a couple of times."

"Could Mr. Hotness be working his way back?" Jade's smile widened with hope.

"Definitely not. I'm leaving in the morning."

"You've always got tonight." She wiggled her eyebrows.

"How are you allowed to teach small children with such a dirty mind?" Ava chuckled.

"I can switch it off in class. A bunch of hyperactive six-year-old kids will definitely put you off the act of procreation. But I always preach about forgiveness, and maybe you're heading that way with Nick?"

Had she forgiven Nick? She didn't think she would've let him touch her if she wasn't heading that way. "I think I am."

"Then go into that bedroom and forgive him."

"Jade!" Laughter bubbled from Ava.

"God, I'm sorry. I haven't had any action for a while and wanted to live vicariously through you."

"I'll admit it's tempting. *God*, it's tempting. But I can't go there again. It's too complicated."

Jade sighed. "Okay." Then she brightened. "I almost forgot to tell you that my cousin Liz got engaged. Things are looking good. They've been together two years and he hasn't left yet.

How good is that?"

Jade believed all the women in her family were cursed. Some witch hundreds of years ago put a spell on all the Brennan descendants and none of the women had had a successful relationship since. Ava thought it was a load of rubbish, but Jade wouldn't hear differently.

"That's great. I'll keep my fingers crossed for them." What else could she really say?

"It's getting late. I'm going to bed." Jade's smile split her face.

"*Alone.*"

The smile dropped. "One more thing before you go. Will you make it to drinks on Tuesday?"

She didn't know what Bella's problem was, plus she didn't know how long it would take to get her car fixed, so she doubted it. "You'll have to Facetime me."

"That will be the first one anyone's missed." Jade sounded disappointed.

"I know, I'm sorry. I'll see you at the next one."

"Okay. Good night."

"Night, Jade."

She was about to disconnect the call when Jade piped up. "Ava? Do you think you can sneak into Mr. Hotness's room, so I can see that gorgeous man one more time? Oh my God, that body!" She fanned a hand in front of her face.

"Good night, Jade." Shaking her head and laughing, she disconnected the call and placed the phone on the counter.

"Nice girl," a deep, sexy voice said from behind her.

Chapter 11

*A*va jumped and held a hand to her chest as she swiveled toward him on the chair. "How long have you been standing there?"

"Long enough to discover your friend's a pervert." Nick chuckled.

He hadn't bothered covering up, and he noticed Ava's gaze drop to his bare chest.

"You shouldn't sneak up on people. It's rude."

"I didn't think I was. I don't tiptoe around my own house."

She frowned. "Why are you up again?"

"Can't sleep. Thought I'd have some warm milk." Ingredients for the makings of hot chocolate were scattered on the counter, and he pointed to the pot. "Any left?"

She nodded, and he walked to the stove to warm the milk back up. While he waited, he propped his hip on the edge of the counter and crossed his feet at the ankles.

This time her gaze traveled from head to toe, or more like chest to crotch. "Don't you think you should cover up?" she asked, waving a hand up and down in his direction.

"When did you become so prudish? We've seen each other in a lot less." It was his turn to do some inspecting, and damn, he wanted to touch where his gaze had wandered.

An eloquent shoulder shrugged, and she tucked a lock of silky, black hair behind her ear.

"Things have changed. We don't like each other that way anymore."

*We don't like each other that way anymore, my arse.* Her gaze devoured his body just as much as he did hers. They liked each other exactly that way. Red-hot lust ignited between them, burning bright whenever they were close. Hell, whenever they were in the same room.

Why wasn't he taking what he wanted? Taking what he knew she wanted too? Was it still because of the way she'd left him? Time had passed; he'd overcome the obstacles she'd left in her wake and had done better for it. And if he was honest with himself, the anger he held onto had subsided over the last two days.

No matter how hard he tried to convince himself he didn't want her, his body rejected the idea. He wanted her all right. Wanted what their bodies could do for each other. They were two consenting adults. Young love had died when she left, and there was no preconception about picking up where they'd left off.

With that sorted in his mind, and the flare of heat

shooting from Ava's eyes, it was time to give each other what they craved.

Nick turned to switch off the stove. The pot had over-boiled and the kitchen now smelled like burned milk.

As he sauntered over to where Ava sat, her eyes grew heavy-lidded, and she rose to meet him. If he had any doubt about whether she wanted to do this too, it left his mind as soon as she placed her mouth on his and trailed the palms of her hands over his chest. She tasted of chocolate and sugar, and he'd never tasted anything so sweet.

A rough sound rumbled deep from his throat, and he gripped her hips, pulling them closer.

She gasped as their bodies connected, and her lips broke free. They stared at each other for a beat, then his lips claimed hers in a hungry kiss. In their frenzied state, Nick slipped his hands under her t-shirt and pulled it over her head.

"God, you're beautiful. I never thought you could look any better."

Her hands skimmed his chest, and he shivered. "You're not looking too bad yourself these days."

Moaning, he dropped his forehead against hers. "If we start this, I don't want to stop. Tell me now if you're not going to continue." *Please God, don't let her stop.*

She stepped back, and he wanted to drop to his knees and yell *why, God, why?* But she slipped her fingers into the sides of her silky undies and slid them inch by sexy inch down her long legs until she kicked them aside and stood between his legs. "I don't want you to stop." His head dropped back, and he stared up at the ceiling.

"Thank fucking God!" She laughed, and the sexy, husky tone sent fire to his already heated arousal.

"But…" she said, looking at him more serious. "This is only for tonight. Nothing more is going to happen."

"Agreed." At this point he'd consent to anything.

The quick reply had her staring into his eyes as if she were searching for the truth. When she must have been satisfied with what she found, she nodded. Then the slow, seductive smile returned. "You're a little overdressed." And she proceeded to slide his boxers down his legs, following the descent.

Once on her knees, she cupped him in one hand and stroked the length of him with the other. When her warm mouth wrapped around him, he hissed and his legs buckled from under him. Locking them in place, he lifted her up by her shoulders.

A dark eyebrow raised questioningly.

"It was going to end super-fast and only one of us would've been satisfied."

"I thought you'd have more stamina in your old age. But if you need a moment to pull yourself together…" Her amusement was clear in her expression.

"Nothing wrong with my stamina," he growled.

"Many men have the same problem—"

He smashed his lips against hers, cutting her off, and cupped her breasts. Her rosecolored nipples pebbled in his hand, and he broke away to suck them into his mouth. She let out a sigh of pleasure and all amusement left her face; in its place was desire and anticipation for what was to come. The need to taste her everywhere was burning him alive, and he lifted her onto the kitchen counter, spread her knees apart, and bent down to place his mouth at her warm center.

Jerking at the contact, she cried out. "Nick... I'm going to..."

Then she shuddered long and hard. She collapsed back onto the counter, covering her eyes with her forearm. Nick stared at the golden goddess sprawled in front of him. It was better than anything he'd ever seen. He chuckled.

"You better not be laughing at me," she said, still not removing her arm.

He tried to wipe the smile off his face, but his lips twitched at the sight of her pout. "I thought *you'd* have more stamina in *your* old age," he teased, slinging her words back at her.

"Oh, you think you're funny?"

She propped herself up on her hands, and his mouth watered as her breasts were mere inches away. Heat coiled low in his belly, and all amusement faded. This woman was slowly killing him.

Stepping closer, he wrapped her legs around his waist and picked her up off the counter. Her arms clung around his neck. Their lips fused together as he carried her into his room, dropped her on the bed, and followed her down.

"Are you going to last a bit longer, Avi-baby?" he said as he kissed her stomach, making his way to her breasts.

"I should slap you for that," she hissed.

"I didn't know you were into S-and-M now," he teased.

"Just shut up and show me if you've improved over the years." She groaned, threading her fingers through his hair.

He pulled away to look at her. "I wasn't good enough for you back then?" Not once had she ever complained.

"You were okay."

"Okay?"

Ava's lips twitched, and she laughed.

"You're going to pay for that," he growled, too aroused to see the funny side at the moment.

"I can't wait," she said, giving him a hot look that singed his skin.

Neither could he. Reaching over to his bedside table, he pulled out a condom, ripped the foil packet with his teeth, and rolled it on with shaky hands. If he didn't get inside Ava soon, he'd explode, and not in a both-get-satisfied kind of way.

They both gasped as he entered her hard and fast. She was warm and ready for him.

Closing his eyes for a moment, he drew in a couple of jerky breaths. *God, she feels good.*

Her impatience showed when she gripped his arse, urging him to move. He didn't need further encouragement, pumping into her as he buried his face in her neck. Her pulse raced fast under his tongue, and she rocked against him, matching his pace, until they both exploded in gasps of long moans and heavy breathing.

They kissed until their bodies stopped quivering, then

Nick collapsed onto his back, throwing his arm above his head.

Tilting his head, he was pleased to see a woman who looked thoroughly sated. "That was better than okay, and damn, I think we got even better with age."

Ava laughed and her breasts jiggled as she turned to look at him. That was all it took for him to get another hard-on.

"I have to agree." Then she cast her eyes to what was happening down south and raised them back to him with an arched eyebrow. "You're ready again so soon?"

"I'm not as old as you think. We have one night, I want to make the most of it." She flashed him a sexy grin.

"Hold that thought." He bounded off the bed and into the bathroom to clean up.

When he returned, she knocked him on his back and straddled him, leaning forward enough for her breasts to hang inches from his watering mouth.

"Ready for round two?" she purred.

*Round two, three, fucking twenty.* But instead of voicing his thoughts, he simply nodded.

"This time I'm in charge," she said as she reached between them and stroked him.

His head tilted back, and he raised his arms above his head in complete surrender and grasped the headboard.

"I love a woman who's in control."

The next day, Ava experienced the morning-after awkwardness she'd always avoided. Never had she spent the whole night in a man's bed or let one stay in hers. But when she tried leaving Nick's bed early in the morning, he'd reached for her hand, pulled her by his side, and proceeded to kiss her until her insides heated into liquid for the fourth time. And all thoughts of leaving vanished.

Now they fumbled around the house, trying not to get within touching distance. When Nick passed her a coffee, their fingers brushed, and he snatched his hand away as if he'd been burned. A tightness gripped at her chest as she took a sip of the hot brew, trying to pretend the simple touch hadn't sent her heart racing.

God, she wished it would stop. This situation, and the effects it had on her body and mind, was something she had no idea how to deal with. Hopefully it would pass as soon as she left the house and stopped thinking about the night before. But what a night it had been. She hadn't had sex like that since… Well, not since she'd last been with Nick, and it had only gotten better. It might actually be hard to forget.

Ava's bag was packed and sitting by the front door, and Nick picked it up, not quite looking her in the eye. "You ready?"

She swallowed the last bit of coffee then nodded, took the mug to the sink and rinsed it. Turning to look at the small, cozy kitchen for the last time, a lump formed in her throat. There'd been so many great memories here. Even the new ones. They may not have begun that way, but they no longer hated each other. Nick's betrayal of the past didn't cut her like it once did. She wouldn't have been able to sleep with him if she held on to old resentment. Maybe they could be friends after all, but if they couldn't...well, her memories of him weren't so bitter.

"Can we stop by and see Maggie before we go?" she asked as they got into the truck. "Sure," he mumbled and drove to Maggie's in silence.

A quick glance at him showed an unreadable expression. Did he regret last night? As awkward as they were acting this morning, she hoped not; she didn't.

Maggie was on the front veranda when they drove up. Shielding her eyes from the morning sun, she smiled as they got out of the truck. Molly barked happily at her from the back of the truck.

"Just in time for coffee," Maggie said as she kissed Nick on the cheek and gave Ava a warm hug.

"We've already had coffee. I'm taking Ava into town. She wanted to see you to say goodbye."

Maggie turned to Ava. "You're leaving so soon?"

Ava laughed. "I think Nick's getting sick of me tagging after him." She glanced at him, but he didn't dispute it. Disappointment tugged at her stomach.

Maggie waved her comment away like she was swatting a fly. "You've most likely been wonderful company."

Ava would have thought so last night, but this morning he was back to barely speaking to her. This was why men weren't worth the trouble. One night with one and it was playing with her mind. She never wanted to be one of those girls pining over a guy, wondering if he'd call.

"I'm not sure Nick would agree," she joked. Then, to change the subject, she added,

"Before I go, I was wondering if I could take some photos of your pictures to show my friend Lauren."

"You were serious about that?" Maggie sounded surprised.

"Of course I was. They're beautiful. I know she's going to love them." Maggie blushed a deep red at the compliment and then ushered Ava inside.

"I'll just wait out here," Nick called after them as they entered the house.

As they walked through the hallway where the photographs hung, Ava pulled out her phone, her attention once again landing on the run-down gazebo. Her heart broke at the image of what was once a beautiful structure and one of her favorite places. But the photograph was gorgeous, and it was the first one she snapped. She ended up taking photos of all of them. They were all so good.

"Brad mentioned he was helping you frame some." She glanced around the living room where they had ended up. "Brad's gone?"

"Yes, he left early this morning. Doesn't like leaving Lexi for too long, especially now that she's pregnant."

"Have you ever considered displaying your work in a gallery?" Ava asked as she thumbed through the photos on her phone, checking to see if she'd missed any.

Leaning a little closer to her, Maggie flicked a quick look to the front door and whispered, "There's an empty shop in town that would be perfect."

She didn't know why Maggie was whispering, but she thought she should too. "And… Why don't you lease it out?"

Maggie's shoulders slumped, and her expression grew grim. "I would love to, but traveling every day from the farm to town and back is too far."

Ava didn't blame her, especially when the weather turned rough like the last two days. "Would you ever consider moving into town? You must be lonely out here now that Paul's gone." Then she slapped a hand to her mouth. "I'm sorry, Maggie. I didn't mean to sound so insensitive."

"It's fine, and you're right, it is lonely. I want to sell the farm and live in town. All my friends are there, and I'd keep busy with the gallery." Maggie's face lit up with excitement, but it was gone in a flash. "But I can't."

"Is it because of all the memories here?" Ava gently asked.

"I can take those memories wherever I go. Yes, it will be hard to leave the farm where I raised my family, but I have no problem leaving."

Ava frowned. "So what *is* the problem?"

Maggie took a deep breath. "Nick."

"Oh." Ava nodded. Where would he work if she sold the farm? But surely there would be plenty of farms that needed good farmers.

"Could he buy it from you?"

Maggie was stopped from answering when the front screen door opened and slapped close. Heavy footsteps tapped on the timber floor as Nick made his way to the living room.

"Ready?" he asked Ava.

"Yep." She turned and hugged Maggie and whispered in her ear, "Go for it."

When they pulled apart, Maggie's eyes glistened with unshed tears. "Promise you'll see me again before you leave town?"

"I promise." Then she followed Nick to his truck.

As they drove away and headed to the main road, Ava glimpsed a white, circular roof in the distance, peeking from amongst the trees, something she hadn't notice when it had been so overcast.

She pointed in the direction. "Can you take me to the gazebo?"

"Why?" Nick threw her a quick, quizzical look.

"I saw a photograph on Maggie's wall. The gazebo's destroyed. I want to see it for myself."

He gave her a curious look but said nothing as he took the dirt road, now muddy from the rain, that led to the gazebo. She didn't know why she wanted to see it in such disrepair, she just knew the desire to was strong.

Deep green pine trees stood like soldiers around it, protecting it like it was in their charge. Well, they hadn't done a good job. What was once gleaming white and solid was now dull and cracked. Timber railings had collapsed into pieces and sat rotting on the ground.

Ava's chest clutched, and she squeezed her eyes closed for a moment, trying to remember its former beauty when flowers of every color grew wild around the perimeter. It was their place to hide away from the rest of the world, especially from her troubles at home.

Getting out of the car, the grass up to her knees, she made her way to the stone steps. She heard the sound of Nick following behind her.

"What happened to this place?" she asked, surprised to hear emotion thick in her voice.

Nick shook a railing, she assumed to test its stability, then leaned a hip on it. "We had a big storm about five years ago. We lost a couple of sheds, and the gazebo got a beating."

"Why didn't you have it repaired?"

"No one was using it, wasn't worth spending the money." He picked off some chipping paint and it crumbled in his hands.

Did he care so little about what was once so special to them? Maybe she'd only been the one who thought it significant. She'd made love to Nick for the first time here. It was the first time she'd ever had sex.

"You took my virginity right on this very floor." They'd had blankets, and with the seclusion from the trees, they felt like the only two people in the world.

Nick's eyes widened, then he shook his head. "You weren't a virgin."

"Yes, I was." When he still didn't look convinced, she added, "I only made out I wasn't to piss off my father." It had been the only way she knew how to hurt him for hurting her mother.

Nick ran a hand through his hair. "Had I known, I never would have..."

"What? Had sex with me? Of course you would have. We couldn't keep our hands off each other."

He gave her a long look. "So, was I a way to get dear old daddy pissed off too?"

She couldn't deny that had originally been her plan. What would make her father blow a gasket more than her dating a poor Williams farmer boy? She nodded, and when he shook his head and shoved away from the railing, she quickly added, "I was going to go on one date with you. It was all I needed to flip Dad out, but one date wasn't enough for me. You were exciting and kind and fun. It didn't hurt that you were freaking hot." She smiled, hoping he could see she was telling the truth.

Blowing out a breath, he chuckled, the deep, sexy sound making her insides quiver.

"Freaking hot, eh?"

"Like, oh em gee so *freaking* hot. I could have died," she said, imitating the voice of a teenage girl.

"You were *freaking* hot back then too. And even hotter now." He sauntered over to her and ran a finger down her cheek.

Her body flushed hot and turned on in an instant, and she tilted her face to receive the kiss she hoped was coming.

She didn't have to wait long. His mouth brushed against hers with feather-light strokes. His tongue darted out and slid along her bottom lip. She groaned into his mouth, and the kiss turned hungry. Stroking his hand along her stomach, his fingers brushed underneath her breasts, and she shivered at his touch.

He broke the kiss abruptly, and she groaned with disappointment. "I want you again, Ava. I don't give a fuck that we said it would only be one night. Right now can be the last time. What do you say? One more for the good ol' days?"

She tried to laugh, but a moan escaped her lips when he slipped his hand in the waistband of her jeans and tugged her closer. The feel of his warm, hard body against hers made her legs tremble. Suddenly, she felt restricted in her tight jeans.

Like he was feeling her frustration, he said, "If I had my way, you'd be wearing that tshirt I gave you 24/7. It was the sexiest thing I'd ever seen."

That t-shirt was now packed in her luggage. It had been so comfortable she didn't want to give it back. Or so she told herself.

He flicked open the top button on her pants, giving his hand better access, and headed south. She could barely stand, because her legs were as wobbly as cooked spaghetti.

"Ava," he growled. "Yes or no?" His breaths came out in shuddery, hot puffs against her neck. Her body exploded with goosebumps.

"Yes," she gasped, threading her fingers through his hair and tugging his head so she could look at his face. His eyes were dark and heated, and she wanted to remember that fierce expression.

They made quick work of their clothing, and Ava welcomed the cool air over her feverish skin. Nick's hot gaze traveled the length of her body, and her blood pulsed with excitement.

Instead of grabbing her and taking her fast, he surprised her by running a finger slowly from her collarbone down to her belly. She shivered. This was going to torture her to death. And what a beautiful way to die.

"I don't have a blanket," he said.

At first her lust-filled mind didn't know what he was talking about, then a moment of clarity hit and she knew he meant using a blanket to lie on. She scanned the floor, then picked up his t-shirt from where they'd tossed it. Spreading it on the bench seat, she motioned for him to sit.

The sexy grin he flashed caused her stomach to do backflips. "You in charge again?"

"Someone needs to be. Now sit."

He didn't argue. Spreading his legs, he pulled her between his muscular thighs, giving him the perfect height to reach her breasts, and he took his time paying equal attention to them both. Blood pounded through her veins. When he reached his hand between her thighs, her already unstable legs buckled beneath her.

Catching her, he straddled her on his lap and continued with his slow, sensual exploration of her chest. Then he nipped her shoulder and palmed a breast and she was lost in the sensation of his caress. Leaning away, he reached down to pick up his discarded jeans. Was he getting dressed? *I'm going to kill him. He can't leave me like this!* But he reached in the pocket, pulled out his wallet, and took out a condom.

She let out a long, shuddery breath. Thank God he was still thinking straight. For the first time ever, she'd forgotten about protection.

The slow smile he gave her was so sure and sexy it made her hot and bothered, and she couldn't wait any longer. Raising slightly, she then lowered herself on him.

"God…" he hissed.

As he moved within her, they kept their eyes locked on each other. When her body exploded, he gripped her hips, thrusting until he found his own release. She collapsed on his chest, her body so weak she didn't think she could ever stand again.

Nick wrapped his arms around her and placed a soft kiss on her shoulder. She was surprised at the tenderness, and her heart squeezed.

When they were stable enough to move, she got off his lap, and they both picked up their clothes and dressed. Smoothing out her hair, she turned to Nick as he was pulling a t-shirt over his head. What a shame to cover such a beautiful body. But as good as his body was to look at, and as amazing as he made her feel, not knowing why he'd betrayed her was always on her mind. If she didn't ask him now, she might never know the answer.

"Why did you do it, Nick?"

He paused as he was putting on his boots and glanced up at her. "Ummm. Wasn't it what we both wanted to do? You looked like you were having a good time."

She waved a hand in the direction of the bench. "No, not that. You…"

"I what?" Boots now on, he stood in front of her.

"You took the money and ran," she blurted.

"I what?" he repeated, his eyebrows boosted into his hairline.

"When my father offered you money to stay away from me, you took it." Why was he pretending to act so surprised?

"You've got it all wrong." His lips flattened.

"My father didn't offer you money?"

He let out a long, low sigh. "He did."

Even though she knew this and thought she'd moved past it, it was still a punch in the gut to hear Nick admit it.

"But I never took the money."

"Dad said you couldn't get your hands on it fast enough."

"I didn't take it." His tone took on a hard edge.

Still not convinced, she said, "The day after you allegedly took the money, I was told you bought Colin Benson's workshop where you worked. How did you get the money if not from my father?"

Hard lines creased the sides of his mouth. "I had enough saved up for a deposit."

"And you expect me to believe that? Colin was known to be a tight arse, he couldn't have been paying you much."

"Believe what you want. Me and Brad worked fucking *hard* to save that money. Why the hell do you think I never took you anywhere nice and we spent so much time on the farm? Because I was busting my arse to find a way to do better for myself. Better for us." He waved a hand between them.

There was something about the intensity in Nick's eyes, the fierce tone of his voice, that Ava believed. Why had she automatically believed he would've taken the easy way out? He was too proud and worked hard. She always knew that. But she'd been looking for an excuse for the guy she was falling for to hurt her; preparing for it. Didn't people eventually get hurt in relationships? Nick had been too good to be true.

"The son of a bitch lied to me!" she yelled, slapped her hands on her hips, and paced the gazebo. "And I believed him."

A flash of hurt passed through his eyes, and it was like a knife twisted in her heart.

"I shouldn't have believed him. I'm sorry." And she was. "Why didn't you come and tell me?"

He sat on the bench and rubbed his palms on his thighs. "He told me you took off to Sydney with Lachlan Ranger."

Her jaw dropped open. "Lachlan Ranger, the real estate guy? He was probably fifteen years older than me."

"He had money and connections in the city. An offer you couldn't refuse." That's what her father had told him.

"But... I didn't..." Her face heated. "If my father was standing in front of me right now, I'd wrap my hands around his neck and squeeze." She slumped down on the bench seat next to Nick. "That's why you looked as if you wanted to kill me at Dexter's."

"Kill is a bit strong of a word."

She laughed. "No, you wanted to. If looks could kill, I'd be dead and buried."

"How am I looking at you now?" His eyes hooded and blazed with pure lust.

She leaned in and kissed him. "Once more for the road?"

"You don't have to ask me twice."

## Chapter 12

Ava hadn't left Nick for bigger and better things with Lachlan Ranger like Bernie had him believe. Nick pondered this as they drove in silence toward town. When Bernie had offered him money to stay away from Ava and he rejected it, he should've known he'd try something else to keep them apart.

Bernie had been keeping something from Ava her entire life, and Nick happened by accident to know what it was. At the time, her father would've done anything to keep it from her. He wondered if, after all these years, Bernie had finally told her. She hadn't mentioned anything, so he wasn't going to ask.

Why had he been so quick to believe she'd left him for someone else? Had he thought so little of her, so little of himself, that he believed she didn't want him for who he was? If he delved too deeply into his past, his answer would most likely have been yes. So he'd spent the last ten years making something of himself. Was it to prove his worth to himself or Ava?

Probably both.

"Am I dropping you off at Greenhill House?" he asked.

Ava had been so engrossed looking out the passenger window, she jumped at the sound of his voice. "No, I called this morning, they're booked up for the next few days."

The bed-and-breakfast he owned was popular. He owed it to Ron and Megan for doing such a great job running it. "So where am I taking you?"

She let out a long sigh, and her shoulders slumped. "I guess I better go to Dad's place. Bella needs me."

"Is everything okay?" he asked.

Shrugging, she rested her head on the headrest and turned to look at him. "Not really sure. Bella wouldn't discuss it unless I came home. Teenagers tend to dramatize things."

"I'm sure you're right."

They drove through the main parts of town, and Ava gazed at all the buildings and shops that weren't around ten years ago. "Wow, Sunland Valley is looking quite impressive. Wait…"

She swiveled in her seat to look back at a caryard they drove past. "That used to be Collin Benson's old workshop. Now it's twice the size and has a caryard."

"That's where your car will be." He had a feeling seeing Collin's old place wasn't what surprised her.

"That's *your* place now? You really did buy the property, and from what I could see, doubled the size." Her eyes widened as she stared at him. He guessed the *Williams* sign written across the building was a big giveaway.

"I can get you a good deal on your tires, but Mercedes parts don't come cheap."

She held up her hand like a stop sign. "I thought you worked on the farm?"

"I'm doing both." But neither were his real job.

"I'm so glad I didn't ruin your business for you. I'm sorry I started such a stupid rumor. It looks great now. Good for you." She beamed.

"Thanks."

He cleared his throat and waited to see if she'd connect the dots and realize his caryard was part of the Williams chain. When she didn't, he didn't bother mentioning it. He wasn't exactly sure why he was still keeping it to himself.

"There's going to be a race day in a few days." He pointed to a banner promoting the day strung up above the street. "Your family will no doubt be there. Will you be sticking around for it?" He'd be there too. His company put the races on. It was a way to direct business into the town and keep Sunland Valley thriving.

"I'm hoping to be long gone by then."

His gut clenched at the thought of her leaving. It had only been three days ago that he would've been happy to see the back of her—hell, he had been ready to escort her away personally. Now he wasn't so eager to see her go. He was sure he would've felt the same way if it had been any other friend he hadn't seen in years. *Yeah, right.*

When they reached Bernie's place, the Cardona Stud Farm, Nick pulled onto the graveled driveway lined with pine trees and drove past green horse paddocks until they reached the main house. He had only been there once, to drop off car keys from Collin Benson. The maid had asked him to wait in the foyer, and he'd overheard a conversation—more like an argument— between Ava's parents that would've shattered her life. Bernie spied him outside his study door, and his relationship with Ava became history.

Nick glanced over at Ava. She bit her bottom lip, looking at the sprawling sandstone house with its pristine gardens like she wasn't in a rush to leave the truck. Again, he wondered if Bernie had ever told her the truth. But it was no longer Nick's business. They weren't in a relationship anymore, and what happened in her family was between them.

"I'll get your bag." He got out of the truck and hoisted her luggage from the tray.

Ava walked up next to him, gave Molly a scratch on the head, and took the bag from him. "Thanks for helping me out these last few days."

He nodded. "Anytime." And he meant it. After learning about Bernie's manipulation he'd let go of the built-up resentment toward her. In fact, he'd let go of it before he'd even learned the truth.

Sliding her hand up his chest, she leaned in and brushed her lips against his. The shocking blast from the innocent kiss broke them apart, and they stood staring wide-eyed at each other. What the hell? He'd had his tongue in her mouth, and on other parts of her body, and he hadn't had quite the same reaction. And from the expression on her face, she'd felt something too.

"See you, Nick." Her breath sounded choppy, and she broke eye contact and turned to leave.

"I'll call you when your car's ready," he said, managing to speak past his tight throat.

She flicked a glance over her shoulder, her smile blinding him. "Thanks."

She rolled her bag toward the entrance, and he watched her sexy hips sway as she walked. He scrubbed his hands over his face then shoved them in his pockets and kicked at the gravel. That woman had him twisted up in knots.

He unclipped Molly from the tray, whistling for her to jump into the now vacant passenger seat. "You're a good girl," he cooed as he scratched behind her ears. Molly's tongue rolled out with pure pleasure. "And extremely less complicated. Come on, let's go fix Ava's car.

The sooner she's out of town, the better off I'll be." But he wasn't sure if he actually believed it.

* * *

Ava placed her fingertips on her trembling lips. Her reaction from that one soft kiss was like a smack to her senses. It hadn't been fueled by lust and desire, but more affection and… She wouldn't use the word love. But something more meaningful than two people wanting to just tear each other's clothes off.

When Nick's truck started and he drove away, she resisted the urge to spin around and watch him leave. She was ready to forget about him. They'd resolved their issues and had a hell of a good time doing so. It was time to move on and ignore the way her body tingled at the thought of his touch.

Before she made it to the veranda steps, the front door flew open. Bella came dashing toward her, with arms wide, a huge smile on her face, and dark, long hair flying behind her.

"Ava!" she squealed and threw her arms around her. "You finally made it."

Ava groaned from Bella's enthusiastic embrace. "Not so tight. I can't breathe."

Bella laughed and let go. "I'm so happy you're here."

"Me too," she lied. Although, she was happy to see Bella.

"How did you get here?" She glanced past Ava, seeking out, Ava assumed, her car.

"Nick dropped me off. My car's going to the workshop."

In a sing-song voice, Bella said, "Ooh, Nick dropped you off."

"What are you doing here?" a gruff voice said behind her.

Ava pivoted around at the sound of her father's voice. His dark hair, threaded with silver, was tousled from the breeze, and his tanned skin had a few more wrinkles since the last time she'd seen him.

"Nice to see you too, Dad." Her fingers clenched and unclenched at her sides. It wasn't the right time to confront him about what she'd learned from Nick. Not in front of Bella. It would probably get heated, and she didn't want to upset her sister.

Bella scuttled over to their father. "I asked Ava to come and visit. Isn't it great?"

Their father didn't know she was coming? She narrowed her eyes at Bella and hoped she read the annoyance in them. Bella ducked her head.

"Yes, it is, just surprised to see you." He took a few steps toward Ava and placed a quick, awkward peck on her cheek. Then demanded to know, "Are you messing around with Nick Williams again?"

Biting her tongue, Ava's lips flattened in a tight line. If Bella hadn't been standing there, looking scared that world war three was about to erupt, she would have some choice words to yell at her father.

When she didn't answer him, he nodded in the direction Nick had left. "I thought I saw him drive away in that old truck of his."

"He was nice enough to offer me a ride," she said as she gritted her teeth. No point telling him she'd spent the past few days *messing* around with him.

"Where's your car?"

"It broke down outside of town."

He pulled out a mobile phone from his pocket. "I'll have someone take care of it."

"No need. It's already done."

"Nick?" A bushy eyebrow raised in question.

"Yes," she said flatly.

Putting the phone back in his pocket, he rubbed his jaw then put a hand on Bella's shoulder, stopping her from bouncing from one foot to the other. "Let's not stand around all day. I'll go tell Olivia to prepare a room for you."

Ava noticed that he didn't say *her room*. He'd probably turned her bedroom into a trophy display for all his prize-winning horses.

Bella seized Ava by the wrist and pulled her to the front door. "I'll tell Mum she's here."

Their father nodded and went to walk away. Then stopped and turned to face them. "Glad to have you home, Ava," he said, his voice gruff. With that, he turned and strode away.

Standing in the warm spring sun, she watched as he rounded the corner of the house and disappeared. She'd been furious about what he put Nick and her through, but for a second, she'd seen a moment of emotion. Something she'd never witnessed from him before. But it had come and gone so fast, she'd probably only imagined it.

"Come on!" Bella tugged her arm.

But Ava stood firm. "Why didn't you tell Dad I was coming?"

Bella shuffled her feet. "Umm… I forgot?"

"You forgot!"

"Yeah, sorry. He's been busy, and I haven't seen him much lately." She tugged at her arm again. "Let's go."

"Okay, okay." She let Bella pull her up the stairs and into the house. Of course their father was always too busy to talk to—nothing had changed.

Once inside, Ava blinked, taking a moment for her eyes to adjust from being outside. She walked into the entrance, her heels clicking on the marble floor, then halted, her gaze scanning the opulent room. Memories came flooding back in full force. Riding around on roller blades when she was ten and hiding the evidence of a smashed expensive vase from her mother that she'd knocked into. Getting caught sneaking into the house in the early hours of the morning by her father and being yelled at for being irresponsible.

Then the one memory she'd forced down into the darkest part of her mind. The night she ran down the wrought iron staircase after her mother, pleading for her not to get into the car. It was the last time she saw her. Her heart shuddered, and she shook her head to clear the image.

Thankfully, Bella had been too preoccupied, petting and talking to the little ball of white fluff at her feet, to notice Ava's trip down memory lane.

"Who's your friend?" Ava bent down to pat the little dog. It rolled onto its back and pumped little furry legs in the air. She laughed. "I suppose you want a tummy rub." And she could have sworn the dog nodded in agreement.

"This is Harry. I named him after Harry Styles. He's my favorite singer and he's so hot," Bella gushed.

Ava laughed.

"Mum's probably in the kitchen." Bella headed off in that direction, and Ava followed.

Bella was right, they found Olivia in the kitchen, elbow-deep in soapy water as she washed dishes. She turned when she heard them enter, and her eyes lit up as her gaze landed on Ava. Shaking her hands from the water and wiping them on her apron, she hurried over to Ava and wrapped her in a warm embrace.

"Oh, it's so wonderful to see you." The top of Olivia's head reached Ava's shoulders, so she reached up and cupped her face and brought her head down so she could place a kiss on her cheek. Then she held Ava's hands, stepped back, and looked her up and down. "Look how gorgeous you are. So grown up. I can't believe you've come home." Olivia's eyes welled up, and she plucked a tissue from her apron pocket to dab her eyes.

"It's nice to see you too," she felt obliged to say, though she'd never given Olivia much thought over the years. She'd been the woman her father had gotten pregnant while married to her mother and then married two months after her mother had been buried. Ava had never formed an attachment to her.

As a teenager, she'd held onto resentment toward this woman who'd invaded her home, trying to take over her mother's place. That's what a girl of fourteen thought. And no matter how nice and caring Olivia had tried to be in those years they'd lived together, she always knocked her attempts of friendship away. Seeing Olivia so genuinely happy and emotional to have her home was a bit of a shock.

"Have you seen your father yet? He will be thrilled to see you." Thrilled wouldn't be what she'd say.

"We just saw him. He wants you to get a room ready for Ava," Bella supplied.

"You're staying?" Olivia clapped her hands. "That's wonderful."

"Only for a couple of days," Ava said. She noticed Bella's disappointed expression, but she'd been away from work for too long. Two days was all she could give her sister. So whatever Bella's crisis was, she'd need to sort it out soon.

Olivia also frowned with disappointment, but said with a smile, "Well, we'll just have to make the most of it. I'll put the kettle on for tea and we can catch up." And she went about filling the kettle with water and getting cups ready.

What was there to *catch up* on? Olivia was more like a stranger than a stepmother. Her father had never brought her along when he'd dropped Bella off for visits. The only time they spoke was when Ava called the house to speak with her sister and Olivia answered the phone. Even then, Ava only made polite small talk. But she smiled and took a seat at the small, timber table. All she really wanted to do was find a quiet place to talk to Bella.

Glancing around the kitchen while waiting for the tea, she remembered the few times when her mother had been sober and taught her how to cook all the Spanish dishes like paella and gazpacho that her father loved but never came home to eat. Her mother soon stopped making dinner and had a housekeeper bring her meals to her room. Ava had never cooked a Spanish meal again.

When tea was ready, Ava told Olivia about her work, her friends, and a few of her interests, much like she'd done with Maggie, but this time her words sounded stiffer, more rehearsed.

Soon they ran out of things to talk about, and Ava rose from the chair. "I'd like to freshen up. What room would you like me to use? And I can set it up, there's no need for you to do it."

Olivia looked at her with a strange expression. "You can use your old room. I'll fetch some fresh sheets for you."

She still had her old room?

Bella followed Ava as they climbed the staircase, chatting nonstop about things Ava had never heard of and people she didn't know, with little fur ball Harry scurrying at their feet. Had Ava ever been that young and carefree? And *chatty*? No, she didn't think so. She'd had to grow up fast.

Did Bella's childhood resemble a fraction of what Ava's had? In all their visits and phone conversations Bella had always given the impression she'd grown up in a happy and loving home, but how could that be with a father like Bernie? Maybe Olivia was good at protecting Bella from what he was really like.

They reached the bedroom, and Ava opened the door. She stopped short in the doorway, and Bella bumped into her. Even Harry gave a little yelp at the sudden stop, then scuttled around their ankles and ran into the room.

The room was exactly the same as when she'd left. The same yellow daisy print wallpaper, the Maroon 5 posters tacked on the walls, even the white, frilly bedspread was the same. Taking a few steps further into the room, she trailed a finger along the pearl white dressing table. All her perfume bottles were lined up how she'd left them. The silver jewelry box sitting on the table wasn't tarnished from age and misuse but shined like it had recently been polished.

Her gaze landed on a glossy, black frame. Her hands trembled slightly as she picked it up. A black-and-white photo strip, the ones taken from the booths in the mall, was inside. Her and Nick's big, goofy smiles beamed from the frame. The photos were playful and fun. Her heart gave a tight squeeze at the young love. A love her father had ruined.

She needed to push her feelings about that down for now and get to the point of why Bella needed her here. Before she could ask Bella any questions, Olivia came shuffling in the room, carrying sheets and towels.

"Let me take those for you." Ava relieved Olivia of the bundle and put them on the fourposter bed.

"I'll just be a minute making up your bed and I'll let you two girls have some time alone."

"That's not necessary. I can manage. But thank you."

Olivia smiled. "Well, I'll leave you to it. Let me know if there's anything you need."

"Will do. Umm, Olivia…" Ava waved a hand to take in the room. "My room is exactly how I left it. Why?"

"It's your bedroom," she answered as if she wasn't really sure why Ava would ask such a question.

"Yes, but it hasn't been for years. Why haven't you changed it into something useful?" Olivia's smile was slow and a little sad. "Your father had always hoped you'd be back. And when it didn't look like you were coming home, he didn't want anything changed." Ava stared at her.

"It's a bit dated now. Feel free to do whatever you like to spruce it up."

"That won't be necessary. I won't be here long enough." If her voice sounded strained, no one said anything.

Olivia nodded. "I'm preparing lunch. Come and join us when you're ready." She pointed to Bella. "Don't forget you're on dishes duties."

Bella flopped down on the bed, Harry yapping and scratching at Bella's legs to pick him up. "Yes, I know," she whined.

"See you both soon." Then Olivia left the room, closing the door.

Her father had thought she'd come back? He never once asked her if she was coming home. Not once!

"So…how was your weekend with *Nick*?" Bella strung out his name, and her eyes grew wide with excitement.

Ava picked Harry up and placed him on the bed. He went belly up again and she obliged him with a scratch on his tummy.

*The best two days I've had in years*, she wanted to say, but instead she said, "It was okay."

"Did you have s-e-x?" She whispered as she spelled out the word.

"Isabella!" Ava gasped. "You're only fourteen, what do you know about s-e-x?" She too spelled it out. It was wrong saying the word *sex* in front of her kid sister.

Bella rolled her eyes. "I'm not two. I do know what it is and how it's done."

"I hope you don't know that from personal experience." Ava would die if she was sexually active.

Bella shuddered. "Nah, sounds too icky. My friend Rachel's older sister has done it, and she told Rachel that it hurt and was messy."

Ava's body went weak, and she dropped onto the bed. "Promise me you won't think about doing anything until you're forty-five." Bella laughed.

"I'm serious. Promise me." She tried putting on her serious lawyer face.

"You're so funny."

Lawyer face didn't work. "Okay, promise me it won't be for a few more years and you *really* have to love the guy."

"Okay, I promise."

Ava heaved a sigh of relief. "Good. Now let's talk about why it was so urgent for you to see me."

Averting her gaze, Bella paid close attention to the non-existent lint on her jeans.

"What's going on?" Ava asked.

"Dad hasn't been feeling well lately," she finally answered.

"Has he got the flu or something?" If she'd called her here to deal with the man-flu, she wouldn't be happy.

"Umm, no, it's worse."

"What is it?"

"He umm…" If Bella kept picking at her jeans, she was going to tunnel through them, though it would match the hole in the other leg.

"Spill it, or I'll ask him myself."

"He has cancer."

"*What?*" Ava snapped as she sprang from the bed. "Why didn't you say so when you called?"

"Because I didn't think you'd care enough to come." She bit her trembling lip, and a stab of guilt for snapping at her pierced Ava's heart.

"Of course I would've come," she said in a softer tone and sat back down on the bed. "I'm not a heartless bitch. How bad is it?"

Bella shrugged. "I think it's bad. I think he's dying."

Ava might not have the greatest relationship with her father, but hearing that he could be dying was like a blow to the heart. "I need to talk to him and Olivia for the details, make an appointment to speak with his doctor."

"No!" Bella cried and latched onto Ava's wrist, stopping her from going anywhere.

Ava stared down at her curiously.

"They don't know I know."

"So how do you know?"

"I overheard them talking about it." Bella's gaze darted away, and Ava wondered if there was something she was keeping from her. Maybe it was just hard for her to talk about.

"If I can't do or say anything, why did you want me to come here?"

"I didn't want to go through this alone. I heard them saying they're going to tell me in a couple of days, and it will help if you're here."

Ava's heart broke for her baby sister. She should have been around more, so Bella wasn't alone so much and dealing with this kind of stuff on her own. Ava knew it wasn't easy growing up like an only child. She pulled Bella in for a hug. "It'll be okay. I'm sure it's not as bad as you think. Dad's as solid as an ox. He'll be fine."

Grayer hair and with extra wrinkles, but he was still as strong and handsome as ever. Not looking sick or frail at all. He could be in the early stages, and if that was the case, maybe they caught it in time and Bella misunderstood.

"What kind of cancer does he have?" Ava asked.

Bella bit the inside of her cheek and glanced around the room as if she was trying to locate the answer written on the walls. "Stomach."

Ava couldn't put a finger on it, but something about Bella's demeanor was odd.

"Do you really have to go in two days?" Bella asked with a sad expression.

She would have been making her way back home already if she hadn't gotten stranded at Nick's. Just thinking about him caused her heart to skip a beat, and she took a steadying breath to get it back to its normal rhythm. God, she hoped that would stop soon.

"If I can reschedule some work stuff, I could probably stay a few extra days. If Dad doesn't mention the cancer, I'm going to have to approach him about it before I leave. I need to know the details."

"Okay, great!" Bella bounced from the bed, waking up Harry who'd dozed off with his legs stiff in the air. "I'm starving. See you in the kitchen." And she raced out of the room. Harry flew off the bed like he was Super Dog and ran after her.

Ava stared at the doorway they'd scurried through, trying to understand what had happened. One moment Bella had been close to tears, and the next second, happy because Ava was staying. She shook her head. "Teenagers."

---

*Crap, crap crap!* The words bounced through Isabella's head as she scurried down the stairs. What was she thinking?

The plan was to get Ava here so she could try to rebuild their family. She was so sick of feeling like an only child. She wanted her sister around more often, but whatever the problem Ava had with their father was keeping her away. She thought if she told her Dad was sick she'd worry about him and forgive whatever problem she had against him. She never thought Ava would ask so many questions. *Dumb, dumb, dumb!* She should have known.

Plonking on the bottom step, Harry nestled on her lap, and she stroked her fingers through his fluffy fur. "What am I going to do, Harry?" He licked her hand as if comforting her.

"She's going to kill me when she finds out the truth."

But she had a few days to figure out a way to get them back together as a family, and when she told Ava the truth, maybe she wouldn't be mad. Her stomach twisted with unease.

"I'll keep my fingers crossed and pray."

## Chapter 13

The table in the main dining room, which Ava's mother had always insisted be set with their finest china for all meals, sat empty. Instead, the small, scarred, timber table in the warm, sunny kitchen held an array of mismatched plates and glasses. A vase of yellow and white wildflowers that grew in the paddocks sat in the center. Not an artful arrangement delivered weekly from the local florist.

Then Ava counted four place settings. Surely Olivia didn't bother setting a spot for her father. He would never stop working in the middle of the day for lunch. He always said it was a waste of valuable work time. There must be someone else joining them.

Bella was already seated, and Harry sat at her feet with a hopeful expression as he eyed the platter of cold meats Olivia placed on the table. Ava stood in the doorway of the kitchen, uncertain if she should really be here. Funny how being away for so long now made her feel awkward in the house she grew up in.

"Is there anything I can help you with?" she asked. She couldn't stand in the shadows all day.

Turning, Olivia smiled warmly and shook her head. "No, honey, everything's ready. Just waiting for your father."

*Father?* They had a better chance of Santa Claus showing up for lunch than her father joining them for any meal. But she kept her opinion to herself as she sat next to Bella. After all these years, wouldn't Olivia be fed up waiting for him? Surely she'd given up hope of him ever taking time away from work to sit for half an hour with the family.

As Olivia placed a basket of warm bread rolls on the table, heavy footsteps sounded behind her.

"Am I late?" The distinctive voice of her father filled the room.

"Just in time, Bernardo. Take a seat," Olivia said, then blushed prettily when he gave her a lingering kiss on the lips.

"Yuck, guys," Bella complained. "Do you always have to be so gross?"

"Yes, we do." He kissed the top of Bella's head, patted her cheek, and sat on the other side of her.

If Ava wasn't completely floored at having her father join them for lunch, watching the display of affection toward Olivia and Bella had totally shocked her to the very core.

Not once had she witnessed a loving gesture between

her parents, only hateful glares and harsh words. Nor had her father ever kissed her as easily as he'd just kissed Bella. The kiss he'd given Ava outside when she'd arrived was so stiff and robotic. Perfunctory, like they'd always been throughout her life.

"All settled in your room, Ava?" her father asked as he piled his plate with salami, ham, and cheese. Cutting open a bread roll, he smothered it with butter and stuffed it with olives. Did someone with stomach cancer have such a big appetite? She needed to google the symptoms.

"Yes. Though it surprised me to see it looking the same as I left it."

He didn't look at her when he said, "Didn't need the room for anything else." And then he cut open another roll, spreading more butter and filling it with the cold meats and cheese.

"Should you be eating all of that?" Ava couldn't help questioning. Stomach cancer or not, all that processed meat, butter, and bread couldn't be good for him.

He paused with a roll to his lips. "Why? What's wrong with it?"

"Dad always gets hungry after he finishes work. Don't you, Dad?" Bella cut in.

He frowned at Bella. "No more than usual."

"Does all the processed meat upset your stomach?"

The frown given to Bella was now aimed in Ava's direction. "Why would it? I've been eating this stuff all my life."

"I just thought it might not sit well now that—"

"Ava stayed at Nick Williams's house for a couple of

days when she couldn't get into town because of all the rain," Bella blurted.

Ava inwardly groaned at her sister's not so subtle change of subject. Once Ava would have had the pleasure of announcing it herself and watching her father's face turn dark red whenever she spoke Nick's name. It was her way of rubbing it in his face. Now, with maturity and a life away from home, she didn't feel the need to do so anymore. She had her own life, and what she did with it was no one's business.

"Is it true?" A red flush crept up her father's neck.

"It is."

"Are you seeing him again? Because if you are, it would be a big mistake."

"Bernardo, honey, Ava's a grown woman. She can do whatever she likes."

"Well, are you?" he asked, ignoring Olivia's attempt at mediating. His Spanish accent was always more prominent when he was mad.

Ava fired Bella a disgusted look for bringing up Nick, and she at least had the good grace to duck her head and look guilty.

Pulling her shoulders back, Ava tilted her chin. "What if I am?" Nope, apparently she couldn't hold back the teenage girl who wanted to rub bad boy Nick in her father's face.

"He's trouble. Stay away."

Ava's head dropped back, and she stared up at the ceiling for a beat before she said, "I'm not eighteen anymore, Dad. You can't tell me what to do."

"You never did what I asked when you were eighteen."

True.

"Maybe you'll begin listening to me now."

Not likely, and him telling her to stay away had the opposite effect, like it did all those years ago. Although, she never needed to rebel to want to spend time with Nick, nor did she now, but her father didn't need to know that.

"I'm a grown woman, Dad. You can't tell me who I can or can't see. I'll make those decisions for myself."

"He's married."

"*Was* married. He's divorced."

"Because he put his wife in a rehabilitation center."

The need to defend Nick grew stronger by the second. "Because she had a drug problem. He's getting her help."

Her father smacked a hand on top of the table and cutlery bounced. "Why do you think she has a drug problem?"

"Bernardo, please calm down. Let's talk about something else."

Again, Olivia's attempt at soothing him fell on deaf ears. Not waiting for Ava to answer, he continued, "Because he drove her to it. Treated her like dirt and only thought of himself. Any story he's told you is a lie."

The word *lie* ricocheted through her skull, and fury bubbled fast and furious in her veins.

"You want to talk about lies? Let's talk about the doozy you told Nick and I ten years ago."

With a clenched jaw, her father's eyes narrowed, and he didn't say a word.

Out of the corner of her eye, she noticed Bella pick up Harry and hug the puppy to her chest. Guilt tugged at her stomach for behaving this way in front of her, but she couldn't back down now.

"You have nothing to say? Well, let me remind you. You offered Nick money to stay away from me, but when he refused you told me he snapped it up and ran. *And* you told him I took off with Lachlan Ranger."

Olivia's eyes grew large with surprise. "Bernardo, is this true?" A vein pulsed in his jaw, and he nodded.

"How could you?" Olivia cried. "What were you thinking?"

His eyes snapped toward his wife. "I was thinking of getting my daughter away from the town's troublemaker."

Ava scoffed. "Oh, please. You could hardly call Nick a troublemaker."

"He wasn't good for you."

"Why? Because he was a farmer's son? That *farmer's son* is doing well for himself these days." By the looks of his caryard and workshop she'd driven past it was true. When her father didn't speak, only stared, she added, "I'm just here for a few days, stay out of my business." Rising, she turned to Olivia. "Thanks for lunch, but I've suddenly lost my appetite." And she stormed out of the house.

Outside, the smell of country air mixed with the scent of horses filled her senses. Tilting her face toward the sun, Ava closed her eyes and breathed in the familiar smells. When things were bad inside, which they frequently were, she always found comfort outside with the horses.

A few of them were out in the paddocks, so she made

her way toward the stables, trying to shake off the resentment toward her father. Even as a grown woman, he was still trying to keep them apart. Warn her against Nick like she was eighteen again. Nothing was going to come out of the reunion with Nick—a beat of regret passed through her at the thought—but she wasn't going to let her father dictate her life.

Stepping onto the cobbled stone of the stables, she took a moment to adjust to the dim interior. The smell of horses and hay was stronger inside, and she drew in a deep breath. She'd missed this place.

The first couple of stalls she walked past were empty apart from fresh hay on the ground and a trough of water. As she approached the next one a beautiful, sleek chestnut with a white stripe down its nose poked its head out and nickered.

"Oh, hello, you gorgeous thing." The name on a golden plaque on the gate read *Giselle*. "Lovely to meet you, Giselle," she said as she ran her palm along the horse's cheek. Then she noticed her protruding belly. "You're going to be a mummy soon. How wonderful. Too bad I won't be around to help."

Disappointment washed over her as she placed a kiss on the horse's velvety muzzle. The only time Ava was ever in the same room as her father without conflicts, arguments, and snide remarks was when a horse was foaling. It was like all the hostility was dropped, and they worked as a team to assist the vet any way they could. The memory simmered down the anger burning in her stomach.

Then a high-pitched whinny filled the stable. Ava's

heart leaped into her throat. The recognizable sound could only come from one horse, but how could it be? She'd been sold. To Ava's amazement, the head of a golden palomino poked out of its stall. "Amber?"

The horse whinnied again as if answering.

Ava ran to the stall, opened the gate, and threw her arms around her childhood friend who she helped birth, break in, and loved more than anything in the world. Laughing, she rubbed her hands along Amber's body. The horse nudged her shoulder and gave a low nicker.

Finding Amber there was a huge surprise. Her father had threatened to sell the horse when Ava told him she was leaving, but she never believed he'd carry out his threat. However, the day she was packing, Amber's stall was cleaned out and empty. Once again, her heart had been trampled on.

Her mind swam with all the emotions that had hit her ever since stopping at Dexter's Pub. It had been one surprise and shock after another.

Everything was so confusing. Coming home and finding her room looking exactly as she left it, Amber in the stall, and her father still warning her against Nick. It was like stepping back in time, and nothing had changed. But things had changed. Her room and horse might still be there, although she had no idea why, but her life had changed. She answered to no one and was free to do what she wanted. Once she approached her father about his illness and helped Bella understand the road ahead, she was gone.

Picking up a brush, Ava began stroking Amber's

cream mane. Her tail swung gently from side to side. Amber always loved being brushed.

The phone in the pocket of her pants buzzed. Putting down the brush, she dug it out and hit the *answer* button. This time her friend Lauren's face beamed from the screen.

"Hey, Lauren."

"What's in your hair?" was Lauren's greeting.

Running her fingers through her locks, Ava found what Lauren was looking at. "It's hay."

Lauren laughed. "A few days in the country and you're looking like a farmer. Or are you rolling around in the hay with the farmer Jade told me about?"

Jade and her big mouth. "No, I'm with my horse Amber." Ava tilted the phone to fit some of the horse's face on the screen.

"Oh, she's gorgeous. So you're at your dad's now? Why did Bella need you so urgently?"

"She thinks Dad has cancer."

"That's terrible! But she *thinks*? Doesn't she know for sure?"

Ava shook her head. "Apparently, she overheard Dad and Olivia talking, but they haven't said anything to her about it. I don't know how serious it is."

"What are you going to do?" Lauren asked.

"I'm not sure yet. Bella doesn't want me to mention anything. She thinks they're going to tell her while I'm here. She's acting a little strange, like she's not telling me everything." Patting Amber on the cheek, she left the stall and walked outside.

"She's young, it must be scary and confusing for her."

"You're probably right." A trainer was breaking in a horse in the round yard close by, and Ava sat on a spongy patch of grass, watching the horse run around in circles.

"So, tell me about this Nick you've been shacking up with. Jade said he's *gorgeous*."

Ava blew out a breath. "I'm sure Jade gave you all the details."

"She did, but I'd love to see how uncomfortable you get talking about romance."

The fierce look Ava threw at Lauren was supposed to be threatening, but it only made her friend laugh.

"All right, all right. Jade's given me enough info to quench my curiosity. But answer me one thing. Is he really as hot as Jade said?"

"Hey, why does my woman need to know about the looks of another man?" Jack, Lauren's husband, came into view in the background, cradling their six-month-old son, and Ava's godson, Ryan.

"I'm only looking out for my best friend's interests." Lauren threw the words over her shoulder. The smile on her face showed just how smitten she was with her husband. And she had every right to be. A sexy ex-football player holding a baby was enough to make any grown woman drool and her ovaries ache.

"Hey, Ava," Jack called out. "How are things?"

"Great. On your lunch break again, are you?"

"He's starting to drive me crazy. He needs to stay at work," Lauren complained with a laugh.

"And you love the way I come home and drive you *crazy*." Jack wiggled his eyebrows suggestively.

"Do I need to hang up and leave you two alone?"

"No," Lauren said.

"Yes," was Jack's answer.

It had been years since she'd seen Lauren so happy. After a terrible childhood and personal struggles, she was finally living the life she deserved.

"Ignore him. He can wait. He won't leave until he has his lunchtime special."

A laugh burst from Ava's lips. "I still can't believe you're talking about your sex life. Boy, how you've changed."

"That's because I've got something good to talk about now."

"You bet you do!" called Jack, who was now out of screen shot but obviously not out of hearing range.

"Well, whatever you're doing to my girl, keep it up. She has a beautiful glow."

"I plan to."

Lauren rolled her eyes. "You two are too much. I'm going to feed Ryan now. If you need me for anything, just buzz."

Then Ava remembered she did need Lauren. She wanted to talk about Maggie's photographs. "Actually, I'm going to send you some photos I took. They're pictures I think you might be interested in selling at your shop."

"Sure, send them through and I'll have a look. Who's the photographer?"

"Nick's mother, Maggie Williams. They're pictures of the farm, and they're absolutely stunning."

Jack's head reappeared on the screen. "The guy you've been shacking up with is Nick Williams?"

"I haven't been shacking up with… Wait, you know Nick?"

"Nick Williams, your mate with the gazillion car dealerships? Is that who you mean?" Lauren asked Jack.

What were they talking about? "He owns a dealership here in town, but a gazillion? Hardly."

"Nick and Brad Williams are the owners of Williams Enterprises. They have car dealerships all around Australia and are now venturing into manufacturing their own vehicles. They're worth millions," Jack supplied.

How did she not figure that out for herself? The caryard with the familiar Williams branding splashed across the building should've given it away. But in her defense, the building wasn't the flashy, sleek ones that were scattered around the country—one just down the road from her office in Brimland Point. The one they drove past still had the old charm of the original building, only bigger and with a caryard attached to the workshop. And Nick not once mentioned he was *the* Williams dealership.

"The bastard." *How could he keep this from me?*

"Ava, what's wrong?" Lauren asked with concern.

The expression on Jack was the complete opposite. A grin split his face. "He's been getting dirty on the farm, pretending he doesn't own a multimillion dollar company, hasn't he? He could never truly shake the country boy out of him."

"Jack, Ryan needs a nappy change. Get on to that, will you?" The tone Lauren used told Jack he'd said too much. When Jack's face left the screen, Lauren focused her attention back on Ava. "Sorry about him. Wouldn't know what was wrong even if it punched him in the nose."

They both knew that really wasn't true. When Jack and Lauren first met, he knew exactly when Lauren needed him and helped her heal from a painful past.

"I've got to go," Ava said.

"What are you going to do?" Lauren asked.

"There's a farmer boy turned lying bastard I need to have a word or two with."

"Maybe you should wait and cool off."

There was no way Ava could sit and try to cool off. No, she needed to get this off her chest. And it needed to be done now.

"Give Ryan a kiss for me. I'll talk to you later." Ava ended the call before Lauren could say another word.

Getting up, she dusted the grass off her jeans and made her way to the garage where her father kept his car collection. Needing something to match her mood, she eyed the red Maserati. Something fast. Marching to the cabinet that held the keys, she hoped he hadn't changed the combination number. And to her surprise, after punching in the code, the door swung soundlessly open.

All the keys were labeled, and she found the one she wanted. Climbing in the car, she turned on the ignition, and it roared to life. The vibrations of the engine rumbled through her body, giving her a quick thrill. But it died just as fast as she thought about where she was headed.

The workshop was where she'd try first. If he wasn't there then, unfortunately, this baby was going to do a little off-roading.

As the car shot out of the garage, Ava had one thing on her mind. Nick. She was a lawyer; she knew plenty of ways to get away with murder.

## Chapter 14

Nick had finished putting in the fuel pump in Ava's car and was washing his hands when Ben sidled up to him.

"You know you don't need to work on the cars whenever you're here. I just needed help the other day because we were short-staffed," Ben said and casually leaned a shoulder on the wall.

"I can say the same to you." Nick took in Ben's greasy, stained clothes. "Don't you have a nice office you like to sit in and bark orders from?"

There was a nicely decked out office with Ben's name on the door that hardly got used. Ben didn't have to work on the tools. Hell, he didn't have to work at all. His share in the company made him a wealthy man. But he was too hands-on to laze around and twiddle his thumbs.

Pushing himself away from the wall, Ben sauntered closer to Nick. "Tell me again how you ended up with Ava's car," he said, ignoring Nick's question.

Drying his hands on a towel, Nick turned and gave Ben what he hoped was a mind-yourown-fucking-business stare.

"Ahh, come on, boss, when I left you at the pub, you were giving Ava the death glare, and now you're fixing her car? You've gotta give me something."

"Don't you have enough to worry about without sticking your nose in my business?"

"I've got no worries."

"I take it Beth hasn't found out about Jane yet?"

"Me and Beth aren't exclusive."

"So she'll be okay with you screwing around with Jane for a couple of days while she was away?"

Clearing his throat, Ben answered, "Why wouldn't she?"

Nick shrugged. "These things spread like wildfire around here. But like you said, you and Beth are only casual. You've got no worries." Slapping Ben on the shoulder, he walked past him and back into the workshop.

No one should know Ava spent a couple of days with him on the farm. Thankfully, the rain had kept anyone from town coming onto the property and seeing her there. The gossip mill ran strong around here, and he'd been the subject on more than one occasion. The rumors about him causing Kate to turn to drugs had only recently subsided. The town was happy to claim him as their very own celebrity, but they were also quick to believe rumors. Cause a bit of trouble as a kid and they didn't let you forget it.

Following him into the room, Ben scratched his short crop of dirty blond hair. "I'm in deep shit, aren't I?"

"You better hope that silver tongue of yours can get you out of trouble."

"I'll be upstairs in the office if you need me. I have a call to make."

Nick shook his head as Ben jogged up the stairs. If anyone could worm their way out of trouble, it was him.

Looking around the shop, there wasn't anything else that needed to be done. He had to wait for Ava's tires to be delivered to finish her car, and Jerry and Chris, the mechanics, had the next jobs under control.

He could go back to the farm, but Percy had already warned him if he stepped foot on the property today he'd shoot him. Everything was under control there too. It didn't seem he was needed anywhere except back at Williams Enterprises. He knew he couldn't leave Brad to take care of everything on his own for much longer. But how could he leave his mother alone on the farm? How could he walk away from something his father worked so hard to build?

And then there was the fierce urge to jump in his car and head back to Ava. He had to keep finding new jobs around the workshop to stop himself from tearing out of there. But now there was nothing left to do, not even a floor to be swept; he'd done that too, the mechanics giving him a questioning glance from time to time.

While Ava was still in town, and their animosity had dropped, why couldn't they spend the time she was here together? Yeah, they'd agreed it was only a one-time thing.

But why couldn't it be more a short-term thing? Then he could finally purge her from his mind and body, because a few hours with her hadn't been enough.

She was all he could think about. The soft sounds she made when his mouth was on her, the quick gasps when he caressed her most sensitive spots, and the long, deep moans when they finally joined. Even her feistiness and strong will was a major turn on. Everything about Ava was unlike anyone he'd ever known. She'd gotten more exciting with age, something he'd never thought possible.

So if they could just spend a few more days together, preferably in bed, he could get his fill and they could both move on.

But she was staying at her father's house, and Bernie wouldn't like him showing up at their door. When he'd dropped Ava off earlier, he'd seen Bernie in his rearview mirror as he drove away, and if Bernie had a rocket launcher handy, he most likely would've aimed it in Nick's direction.

No, he couldn't go back there.

As he pondered what to do, a sleek Maserati sped into the workshop. *What the fuck does this idiot think he's doing?* Even the mechanics shook their heads at the new arrival.

Getting ready to blast the moron, Nick stormed over to the car just as the door flung opened and Ava got out, her plump lips curled back in a snarl and her nostrils flared. Slamming the door shut, she stomped the few steps toward him and jabbed him in the chest with a sharp fingernail.

"How dare you lie to me?" she spat.

That shook him out of his surprised stupor at having Ava arrive there like a Formula One driver. "You'll need to give me some details about what I've lied about."

"Don't play dumb with me. Your simple *farmer boy* act isn't going to work anymore."

Leaning a hip against the bonnet of the car, he crossed his arms over his chest. Her fiery gaze dropped for a beat to his chest and down the length of him. The clothes he'd thrown on weren't anything fancy. Working on cars got dirty, so he'd flung on an old, faded pair of jeans and a black t-shirt that had seen better days. For a moment he thought she'd given him an appreciative glance, but it was soon replaced with hellfire shooting from her eyes. And she was hot as hell.

"You've got ten seconds to explain what your problem is or I'm going to kiss you."

Sucking in a sharp breath, she bit her bottom lip, and her gaze dropped to his mouth.

Fuck it, he couldn't wait. He stepped forward and reached out a hand.

Before he could take hold, she slapped his hand away and shook her head. "Don't you think about touching me."

Nick let out a long breath. "Is the ban temporary or permanent? 'Cause it will suck for both of us if it's permanent."

Narrowing her eyes, she slammed her hands on her hips, her chest heaving. This time it was Nick's turn to trail his gaze over her body. She was still dressed in the jeans and top she wore this morning, and he knew what was under them. The pleasure of removing each item of clothing was like unwrapping the greatest birthday present in the world. He got hard just thinking about it.

"You think lying to me is a joke? After what we discovered my father did to us."

Okay, it didn't appear she was going to calm down anytime soon. He needed to settle this problem with her and move onto more important things. Getting her in his bed.

"Ava, can you please tell me what's gotten you so upset?"

"You lied!"

"Okay, we've already established that, but can you be more specific?" He had a suspicion as to what it could be. He was surprised she hadn't figured it out sooner. Or maybe her father had told her yet another doozy to keep them apart.

Pacing in front of the car, she took a deep breath and said, "You're not a farmer boy or a mechanic."

That little secret lasted longer than he'd expected. Although, now he couldn't recall why he had been so eager to keep it from her.

"Technically, at the moment, I'm both."

Scoffing, she swung around and glared at him. "Oh, please. Don't patronize me. Why did you lie?"

"I didn't lie."

The hands that were on her hips dropped to her sides. "Lied by omission then."

Well, when it was put that way... Noticing the mechanics had stopped working and stared openly at them, he placed a hand on her shoulder and tried to guide her toward the reception area and out of sight. But she shrugged him away and didn't budge.

"I told you not to touch me."

Briefly closing his eyes, he took a deep breath. "We have an audience. Can we discuss this somewhere more private?"

She glanced at the men, who quickly spun around, filling the room with banging noises.

She nodded and followed Nick into the next room.

When he turned to face her, she was tapping the toe of her shoe, her eyebrow was raised, and she glared at him again like he was scum under her shoe. He scrubbed a hand over his face while she waited for an answer.

What should he say? He'd kept who he'd become from her because he thought she left him because he was a broke farmer. It was what he'd believed all these years, and having more money in his bank account wasn't what he wanted to attract her with.

"You'd left with Lachlan Ranger."

Ava shook her head. "No, I didn't. You know that."

"I know that *now*. I didn't know it when you first came back to town."

Confusion lined her face. "So?"

"He had money that I could only dream about."

The confusion deepened. "Nick, you're not making any sense. What does Dad's lie and Lachlan's money have anything to do with who you really are?"

"For years I believed you ran off with Lachlan because of his money and because he could give you the life I wanted to but was way out of my reach. So, when I saw you at Dexter's, the old hurt and anger came flooding back to the surface. I thought if you knew I wasn't a poor farmer anymore, you'd be attracted to my money." God, it sounded worse out loud than it did in his head. But Ava wanted to know, so there it all was.

She stared at him with a blank expression, not saying a word. He couldn't tell what she was thinking.

"This all comes back down to Dad's lie." She blew out a breath. "But how could you believe I'd leave you like that for a rich guy?"

"How could you believe I'd take a bribe from Bernie?"

She nodded. "We were crazy about each other but didn't have much trust."

"No, we didn't," Nick agreed and sat on the edge of the desk.

"I can understand why you were hesitant about telling me at first, but I thought we moved past the hostility. Why didn't you tell me later?"

She took a few steps closer, and when he reached for her hand she let him take it. Nick answered, "We only found out the truth this morning."

"What about when we drove past this place today? You could've told me then, Nick."

He shrugged. "By that time, you were anxious about going home. I didn't think it was important."

Examining his face for a moment, she must have been satisfied with his answer, because she smiled warmly. She slid in closer and settled between his open legs. Placing her arms around his neck, she nuzzled him below the ear, and heat shot straight to his happy place.

"I don't want or need your money," she said. "I have enough of my own."

"Good for you," he said, dropping his head back as she trailed her warm tongue along his rapidly beating pulse.

"And whatever this thing is that we have going, it's obviously not going to be a one-off, but it's still only temporary—only while I'm in town. So I'll never have any claim to whatever you have."

"I'm okay with that." He was ecstatic to know they were on the same page.

Sliding his hands down her back, he grabbed her hips, rubbing her against him, and a shaky breath slipped from her lips at the contact. Exploring hands skimmed down his chest and into the waistband of his jeans, and the muscles in his body tightened. Damn, Ava could turn him on in a second. If her hands found what he was sure they were in search of, he'd take her right here on this desk. It took all his self-control to clasp her wrists and pull them away.

Frowning, she groaned her annoyance.

"As much as I want to be inside you right now, I don't think I want Jerry and Chris listening."

She stepped away, adjusted her top, and combed her fingers through her hair. "You're right. So tell me, Nick," she said with a cool demeanor, as if they hadn't wanted to rip each other's clothes off only seconds ago. "Why are you getting your hands dirty on a farm and workshop? Shouldn't you be running a corporation?"

He pushed himself off the desk. "After Dad died I needed to take care of the farm. I only come to the workshop when needed."

"You've been here that long?"

He nodded.

"Isn't Percy able to do it?"

Yes, Percy was more than able. "Mum needs me here."

"Maggie's doing so well selling her photos and keeping herself busy, maybe she might like to leave the farm and be closer to town near friends."

A niggling sensation prickled the back of his neck. His mother had mentioned selling the farm once before, but he'd dismissed it. Now Ava was suggesting she might want to move into town. Before he could respond, Ben strolled into the room, grinning from ear to ear when he spotted Ava.

"Look who's here, Ava Cardona, all grown up and prettier than ever." Ben's gaze traveled over her from head to toe.

Ava narrowed her eyes like she was trying to place where she knew the man from. Then her eyes grew round. "Ben? Ben McDermott? It can't be. You used to be…"

"A skinny geek? I filled out all right, didn't I?" He held out his arms and spun around.

Ava laughed and gave him a once-over similar to what Ben gave her. "I'd say you filled out rather nicely."

Ben had been the high school geek. Though he hadn't been into computers and high-tech gadgets, he'd pulled apart engines, building them back again, only faster and louder. The nickname came about because he was as thin as a bean pole and wore thick-lensed glasses. After discovering the gym and having Lasik surgery, he could never be mistaken for a geek again.

"I see you've kissed and made up with the boss," he said, pointing to Nick.

"Nick's your *boss*? You might need to explain that. I'm not sure exactly what Nick's occupation is anymore."

Sauntering closer to her, Ben's voice deepened. "Maybe we can catch up with a drink tonight?"

Blood pounded in Nick's temples at Ben's obvious flirting. Gritting his teeth, he managed to snarl, "How did Beth take the news about Jane?"

Turning back to face Nick, Ben didn't appear worried about his harsh tone. He actually gave him a teasing smile, like he knew he was fucking with his mind. "Beth knows my heart belongs to her."

"It's your dick she doesn't have control over," Nick added.

Ben shrugged. "Speaking of my favorite body part, I promised Beth I'd stop by. The phone sex we just had didn't satisfy her as much as the real thing."

"Too much information, Ben." Nick looked over at Ava, and she was silently laughing.

She probably thought Ben was joking.

"I better not keep her waiting. Great to see you again, Ava." Leaning in, he planted a long kiss on her cheek, extremely close to her mouth, and placed a hand on her hip.

A burning sensation grew in Nick's chest, and he wanted to ram his fist in Ben's face for touching her. Why? He had no idea. Ava wasn't his to claim. She could touch and kiss whoever she wanted. The burning sensation exploded at the thought. Fuck no. While she was in town and they were going to continue whatever the hell they were doing, she was his.

When Ben broke away from Ava, he gave Nick an exaggerated wink. "See ya, boss."

After he left, Ava said, "Wow, he's broken out of his shell, *and* his body. I can't believe that's geeky Ben. He's one good-looking guy and knows it too by the looks of things."

Taking her by the shoulders, Nick swung her around to face him and slammed their bodies together. She gasped, but her eyes simmered with desire as she looked at him. God, that was exactly the way he wanted her to look at him, and only him.

"If we're going to be together while you're here, there's going to be no one else. And stay away from Ben."

Not that Ben would pursue Ava. Nick knew the flirting had all been an act to piss him off, and it worked.

"You can't tell me what to do." She tried pulling away, but her movements were weak and as unconvincing as her words.

Lowering his head, he placed a soft kiss on her lips then pulled away. It took a moment for her eyes to flutter open. "It will only be you and me."

"Like I said, you can't tell me what to do."

He kissed her again, this time firmer and longer, and her body quivered against him. "Tell me."

She sighed and rolled her eyes. "It's not like I have much time to build up a flock of men in the few days I'm here."

It wasn't exactly an agreement, but it was her way of doing what he asked without giving away her power.

She stared longingly at his mouth, like she wanted the kiss to continue, but she stepped out of his arms. "I have to go. Dad might be worried I've stolen his car."

"He doesn't know you've taken it?"

"No, so I better return it before he calls the cops and reports it missing." She laughed, but the amusement didn't reach her eyes. He had a feeling she didn't want to go back.

"Come over later. We can have dinner, and you can stay over."

"It's tempting, but I need to spend as much time with Bella as I can. I'll try to come by later tonight after she's gone to bed. I'll see if I can steal another car."

They walked back into the workshop. "I have a yard full of them, take your pick."

"Thanks, but I don't want to have to explain to Dad how I got it."

"Years ago you would have rubbed it in his face."

Opening the car door, she slid onto the leather seat. "I don't seem to care what he thinks anymore."

Then he remembered why Ava was in Sunland Valley in the first place. How could he have forgotten to ask why Bella needed her here so urgently? With a hand on the roof of the car and the other on the open door he asked, "What was Bella's emergency?"

"Dad has cancer. They haven't told her yet, but she overheard them talking about it. She wants me with her when they break the news."

"How bad is it?"

"I'm not sure. He looks well, and he has a healthy appetite. I don't know if Bella got the information right."

"You haven't talked about it with him?"

The shadow of the roof filtered across her eyes, but it wasn't enough to mask the skepticism. "Bella doesn't want me to say anything yet. There's something strange going on."

"I'm sure you'll sort it out." With that, he gave her a quick kiss and closed the door.

Watching her reverse out of the shop, his heart banged behind his ribs. It hadn't beat so hard and fast since they were together ten years ago. Giving himself a shake, he decided to go for a walk. It was probably only the excitement of having Ava in his arms and not being able to do anything about it that had him feeling so jittery.

The street outside the workshop was buzzing with traffic and pedestrians. With no direction in mind, Nick followed the footpath with the magnificent mountain range as the town's background. The afternoon sun shone golden light through a dusting of cotton ball clouds, striping the landscape with shining rays. Nick found himself smiling at such a beautiful day spread out in front of him. Or maybe he was smiling because of the woman he just had in his arms. Yeah, she sure put a spring in his step.

How did his feelings for Ava come full circle in only a few days? Nick had been ready to leave her stranded in the middle of a storm with only the cows for company. Now he looked forward to when they would meet again.

Even before he'd found out about Bernie's secret, she'd crawled under his skin and occupied his mind...and in a good way. And they knew where they stood in terms of what they wanted. A temporary affair ending when she left town. No one got hurt, and they could remain friends and be on their merry way. Perfect. In theory it was every man's fantasy, but why did his gut twist at the thought of Ava walking away…again?

Before he could think further about it, he came across an empty shop. But what made him stop short was his mother walking out of it with Phil, a real estate agent. The smile on his mother's face as she talked to Phil dropped the moment she saw Nick standing a few feet away.

"Nick… Hello, sweetheart." A stiff smile was put into place, and she said a quick goodbye to Phil.

Nick nodded a greeting to the agent and waited until he left. "What are you doing looking at an empty shop?"

"I'm considering leasing it for a gallery for my photos."

It left him speechless for a beat. He knew she loved photography but didn't think she took it seriously enough to want to lease out a shop.

Giving himself a mental shake, he peered through the grimy window into a dark, dingy space. "Since when have you wanted to own a gallery? And why in a shop like this?"

Her laugh sounded a little high-pitched and forced. Clasping onto his arm, she guided him away. "Let's get a coffee and I'll explain."

Finding the closest café, they chose a table with some privacy. A waitress took their order and scurried away. The café was small but busy enough to be noisy. Nick had a feeling he'd need the noise to muffle his reaction to whatever his mother was about to say.

Watching her fiddle with a tiny silver bucket of sugar on the table, Nick had a sick feeling he wasn't going to like what was coming. Especially because she'd avoided eye contact since they'd sat down.

"Mum, what's going on?"

She stopped fidgeting, placed her hands in her lap, and took a deep breath. "I want to open a gallery to sell my photos."

"Okay, you've mentioned that, but why do you need a shop? Especially a dingy one? I thought you were doing well selling them online."

"The shop only needs a good clean and a lick of paint. It's perfect for what I want. And yes, I am doing well selling them online, but I want something that keeps me busy and out of the house."

The waitress arrived with their coffees. Once the cups were placed on the table and she went on to the next customer, Nick continued with the conversation. "I thought the farm kept you busy."

"Not so much anymore. Percy and Kev do a great job

taking care of things, and they hire farmhands when they need extra help."

Nick shook his head. "I didn't mean the labor stuff, but the books and ordering."

She gave Nick a small smile. "You've been doing that for me, and Percy has too. Besides, I never liked doing that stuff. I only did it because it helped your father."

Okay, starting a new hobby didn't sound so bad, so why did his mother look as if she was about to do a runner? "If you're going to be traveling more often into town, I'm going to give you a new car. Yours isn't reliable enough."

She waved a hand in dismissal. "There's nothing wrong with my car. It's only six years old."

"Exactly, it's too old. It could break down, and you'll be stuck who knows where. I have a car in the yard that will be perfect."

His mother took a sip of coffee, her hand trembling slightly. When she placed the cup on the table she reached across the timber and clasped his hand. Here it came, the bomb he'd been waiting for.

"Nick, I'm not going to be doing a lot of traveling, because I've decided to sell the farm and move into town."

The quietly spoken words blasted in his head. *Sell the farm?*

"No." His response shot out like a bullet, and his mother jumped. Guilt squeezed at his chest for sounding so harsh. Taking a deep breath, he tried to gentle the tone of his voice. "No, you really don't want to sell the farm."

Clasping her hands, she placed them on the table. "I know this is hard on you. But I think it's for the best."

Nick scrubbed a hand at the back of his neck. "You don't want to live there anymore?"

The sad eyes staring back at him gave him the answer. "You don't like living on the farm without Dad."

A tear slid down her cheek, and she quickly brushed it away. "There are too many things that remind me of your father. And being out there all alone I constantly think about him. Some days I feel like I can't breathe because I miss him so much."

"But you're not alone out there, you've got me." But how much time had he actually spent with his mother while he'd been home? Between working on the farm and at the workshop, not much. "Okay, I understand why you want to relocate, but you don't have to sell."

"I have no use for it."

"Then I'll buy it."

His mother gave a small laugh. "And what will you do with it? You have enough business of your own, which by the way, you should be getting back to," she said, giving him a stern look.

"Maybe I need a change. I could run the place full time."

She shook her head. "You will do no such thing. Farming isn't for you."

"But it was for Dad, and he loved that place."

"Yes, *he* loved farming, not you."

"I owe it to him to keep it running."

She held up her hand like a stop sign. "You don't owe your father anything. Why would you say that?"

Blowing out a long breath, he slumped back into his chair. "I should've been around more before he died. Maybe if he'd had more help he wouldn't have had a heart attack."

"Oh, Nicky." The tears were back as she reached across the table to take his hand again. "That was not your fault. You couldn't have prevented it. Do you hear me?" Her tone was fervent.

He heard her, but it didn't stop him from thinking otherwise.

She squeezed his hand. "Your father was so proud of what you and Bradley had achieved."

"Brad managed to find the time to come visit more often."

"Your brother had no reason to stay away. You did."

"What are you talking about?"

She gave him a warm smile. "You lost the love of your life in this town. Your poor heart got shattered. The memories here were tough on you."

He shifted in his seat. "I got over it," he said, ignoring the tightness in his chest.

"My darling boy was head over heels in love, and you didn't just *get over it*. Trust me, a mother knows these things. And I couldn't help but notice a little spark between you two again."

"We've settled our differences, if that's what you mean."

"Have you kissed and made up?" she asked, looking at

him hopefully.

"Mum!" He laughed. "Stop being so nosy."

She shrugged. "Just asking. But seriously, go do what you do best, and that involves cars not cows. You're shouldering guilt you shouldn't be feeling."

It had been coiled in his gut for so long he wasn't sure he knew how to let it go. But having his mother tell him his father was proud of him was a start. As much as it killed him to know his mother wanted off the farm, he understood completely why she needed to leave. The emptiness of his father's absence echoed around the fields, but he couldn't let her sell it to just anyone.

"I still want to buy it."

"No, sweetheart. We all need a clean break. I've offered it to Percy and Kev, and they want to buy it."

"I bet you're practically giving it away to them." They were like family, and his mother would do anything to help them out.

"I don't need much."

"I'm still giving you a new car."

She opened her mouth to argue, but he stopped her.

"*And* I'll buy you the space you want for your gallery. I don't want you wasting money on rent." Crossing his arms over his chest, he continued. "I assume you have a house in mind?" Leaning back on the chair, she crossed her arms over her chest, mirroring his posture.

"I'm old enough to take care of myself. I don't need you to spend your money on me."

"I know you can, and you will, *after* I set you up with what you need. I don't want you to argue about it or I'll involve Brad in this too." At his mother's long sigh, he asked, "Where's the house you've been looking at?"

She tried to stare him down with a disapproving glare, but eventually she gave in and threw up her hands. "It's the miner's cottage on Willow Avenue."

He knew the one, and the owner, and he'd buy it for her.

As they left the café, his mother turned to him and hugged him tightly. "Thank you."

"What for?" He was the one who should be thanking her for giving him what he needed to weaken his grip on the farm and the guilt at not being there for his father.

"For being a wonderful son. A son a mother and father can be proud of."

Wonderful wouldn't be the word he'd use, but he hugged her back and said, "Thanks for being the greatest mother."

Pulling away, she tapped him lightly on the arm and gave a watery laugh. "Now go take care of your own business. And maybe go get the girl." Waving, she hurried across the street before he could respond.

There was still much to do there before he could leave. Buying his mother a house and work space would take a little time. Getting the girl was high on his to-do list also, but not the way his mother intended. No, a few more days in his bed and he'd be ready to let her go back to her own life, and he'd finally get back to the company. In theory, it all sounded perfect. But how would he feel when he watched her walk away? This time they knew where they stood, so he had nothing to be worried about.

Chapter 15

*L*ying on top of the old, frilly bedspread on her bed, Ava stared up at the ceiling. Dinner had been another awkward occasion. Ava and her father didn't speak while Bella and Olivia chattered like old hens to fill in the tense silence. It again surprised her that he bothered showing up for the meal, and she'd watched as he devoured steak, potatoes, and had an extra helping of apple crumble for dessert.

When she got back to her room, she googled the symptoms of stomach cancer, and he showed no signs of having the disease. Either Bella got her wires crossed or she had masterminded this scenario for some reason. She concurred it was the later. Tomorrow she'd get to the bottom of it. And if she had to go ask Olivia or her father, she would, whether Bella liked it or not.

Picking up her phone, she opened the message Nick sent an hour ago.

*Get your sexy arse here so we can continue what we started.*

They hadn't done much in his office, but it was enough for her body to quiver. Usually when she wanted a guy, it didn't matter where they were. Club bathrooms were always popular. But Nick stopped it from going further because they were at the workshop, and it surprised her that she was happy about it. Sex with Nick wasn't something she wanted a shop full of mechanics overhearing. It was something she only wanted to share with Nick. A knot tightly twisted in her chest. She rubbed her hand over it to try to release the tension, and felt the fast pace of her heartbeat.

Quickly sitting up, she wiped the heels of her hands over her eyes. Nick was a friend with benefits, nothing more. A couple of days with him wasn't going to alter her opinion on relationships. She never chased after a man and wasn't going to start now. It was why she was still in her room and not at Nick's place even though her body wanted her there. He'd asked her to come over, and she'd told him she'd try. But she never made plans with men—that came under the relationship category. What was she thinking when she'd suggested spending time together? It was so unlike her.

Obviously, she hadn't been thinking when Nick's hands were on her body. It was never enough with him. Well, it had to be. She'd made a big mistake suggesting they continue seeing each other while in town.

When the phone rang, she wasn't surprised to see Nick's name illuminated on the screen. The temptation to ignore it was strong, but now was as good a time as any to tell him she'd changed her mind. Telling him over the phone instead of face-to-face would be best. *Because you're a big chicken.*

"Nick," she answered.

"Have you stood me up?" She could hear a light teasing in his voice.

"I never promised to come by. I said I'd try." But she'd purposely stayed in her room.

"Well, what are you doing now?"

Sighing, she got up from the bed and paced the bedroom, the plush carpet soft under her bare feet. "It's late, I'm not coming over. Nick, I need to tell—"

"It's a good thing I've come to you," he said, cutting her off.

"What do you mean you've come to me?"

There was a soft tapping sound against the glass of the bedroom window. Pushing back the curtains, she slid open the sliding door and walked out onto the balcony and into the cool evening air. Nick was getting ready to pelt another rock. When he saw her, he dropped the pebble and grinned.

"Just like old times, eh?" she said.

A smile tugged at his lips, and she couldn't help smiling back.

"If my dad caught you here, he'd still shoot you," she said into the phone.

He waved an arm. "Then you better come down here before he catches me."

Nibbling at her bottom lip, she took a moment to

decide what to do. It was silly to tell Nick things couldn't go further on the phone while he stood only meters away. Making up her mind, she said, "I'll be right down."

Stuffing her feet into a pair of Ugg boots that were still in her wardrobe, along with some of her old clothes, Ava snatched the throw blanket off the bed, wrapped it around her shoulders, and hurried down the stairs. As quietly as she could, she unlocked the door and slipped outside.

It really did feel like old times.

Dashing around the corner of the house, she slammed into Nick. He caught her by the shoulders to stop her from falling. Had she sprinted outside so quickly because she was eager to end things or because she was excited to see him? The latter was the truthful answer.

A light flicked on in an upper bedroom, and Nick covered his lips with a finger, grabbed her hand, and led her on quiet feet away from the building. Stealthily, they ran through the dark, just like they used to. Years melted away and she was the same young woman in love with the farmer's boy.

A gasp escaped from her mouth. The 'L' word, and the feelings it pulled up with it, froze her on the spot. The word slammed into her heart like a sledge hammer, trying to break free. Anxiety spread through her chest. It was only the memories of the past that had her feeling this way, right?

"What's wrong?" Nick searched her face.

Hopefully she didn't look as shocked as she felt. "Nothing." She ducked her head so he couldn't read too much into her expression. "I think we're far enough away from the house."

The iridescent glow of the moon shone a pale light through the maple trees they were standing under, and a soft whinny came from the stables close by. It was then she got a closer look at Nick. The stiff smile on his face didn't reach his eyes. Acting on instinct, she held onto his hand and stepped closer. It was her turn to ask the same question. As she stared at his face, pain poured from his eyes, and he swallowed hard, like he needed to clear his throat.

"Mum wants to sell the farm."

"Oh, Nick. She did mention she was thinking about it." Her shoulders sagged over his obvious heartbreak.

"I had a feeling she might have spoken to you about it."

"She didn't say much, but she's lonely there by herself."

"I told her I'd stay."

"You did?"

"I can't imagine not having my parents there. If it meant she'd stay, I'd stay with her," he said.

That sounded like more than sadness at seeing your childhood home being sold. "Why are you having trouble letting go?"

For a moment, he just stared intently into the night, and she didn't think he was going to answer. But then he ran a hand through his hair and said, "It's all that's left of him." She knew he was talking about his father.

"Oh, Nick." She placed a hand on his chest, caressing

above his heart. It shook under her palm. "Your father isn't the piece of land. He's part of you, Brad, and Maggie."

"But he loved that place."

"He loved his family more and would want you to be happy. The farm isn't making Maggie happy, and is it really making you happy?"

Staring into his eyes, she wanted to see the truth when he answered, but he averted his gaze and hesitated a moment. "I could be happy," he finally said.

Cupping his face, she forced him to look at her. "Would it *really* make you happy?"

"No, it wouldn't," he replied, answering honestly. He began caressing his hands over her shoulders and along her arms. The blanket she had hastily wrapped around her when she went rushing from her bedroom slipped off and pooled at their feet.

A shiver ran up and down her spine, and not because of the cool night air. It was because of the man standing in front of her. The raw emotion projecting from his gaze tore at her heart.

The decision to let the farm go must have torn him apart.

She couldn't bring herself to end things with him tonight. Not when his heart was ripped open. And before she was ready to let him go, she needed him one more time.

Continuing to stroke his hands slowly on her arms, his touch caused her body to ignite with a magnitude of sensations, most of them targeting all her good spots.

When he stared down at her with heat blazing from his eyes, her heart fluttered frantically, like a caged bird behind her ribs.

Ava stepped closer and pressed up against Nick, and his eyes darkened with something more powerful than lust. She didn't know what it meant, nor did she dare to analyze it. So, she trailed her hand to his good spot, cupped him, and was pleased to see his eyes turn hungry and almost roll to the back of his head. That was the look she knew how to deal with, and she planned to keep it there.

Taking care of his buttoned fly, Ava slipped her hand in his jeans. Nick growled his pleasure. But before she could continue with her exploration, he removed her hand, brought it to his mouth, and kissed the palm.

Then, stepping away, he picked up the discarded blanket and spread it on the fragrant, soft grass. Kneeling, he held out his hand for her to join him. With a hesitant step, she placed a trembling hand in his strong, steady one and knelt next to him. There was something about the way he watched her that was different from the last few days, and it scared the hell out of her.

She shivered.

"Are you cold?"

She shook her head. "Doesn't this remind you of an old horror movie when the canoodling couple gets attacked by an ax-wielding maniac?" she said, trying to lighten the mood. Why did she feel like such a nervous virgin? When Madonna's song *Like a Virgin* started playing in her head, she knew she'd officially lost the plot.

"If we hear a noise, I'll send you to take a look. It's always the poor guy who's murdered first. Let's change it up." He laughed.

The laughter soon died when he slipped the strap of her top off her shoulder and placed firm lips on her heated skin.

Lost in pleasure, she dropped her head back and her eyes drifted closed. Gentle kisses nipped at her shoulders, neck, and then claimed her mouth with a deep, drugging, curl-your-toes kiss. Her heart picked up in speed and she could hear it thumping in her ears. Could Nick hear it too?

Moonlight, like fairy lights, filtered through the leaves of the tall trees they sat under, and it was too sweet and romantic for Ava to take. So she tugged frantically at the fly of his jeans and yanked them down as far as they'd go and nudged him so he fell on his back. She tried to straddle him, but he drew her down and rolled her onto her back, pinning her under the weight of his firm body. And he began to torture her with slow, gentle caresses.

She couldn't take this tenderness, not when she knew she had to walk away.

"Please, I need you now." The words came out in a strangled whisper. His leisurely exploration was going to kill her.

Either he didn't hear the desperate plea or chose to ignore it, because his hot mouth nibbled at her neck and his hand palmed her breasts, ripping a long moan from her lips.

Soon she was so lost to his slow manipulations she

withered under him, forgetting about wanting things to move quickly and reveling in the unhurried ecstasy of his touch.

"I need you so much." The expression on his face was so passionate she had to bury her face in his neck so he wouldn't see just how much he was affecting her.

What the hell was wrong with her? She couldn't take all these emotions ramming through her body; her heart didn't know where to place them. But one thing she did know where to place was growing impressively against her thigh.

Taking control of the situation, Ava positioned herself, squeezed his hips, and guided him to where she needed him.

With a rough growl that vibrated through to her core, Nick dropped his head on her shoulder and didn't move. Their heavy gasps of air were the only sounds in the still night.

When he slowly began to shift, the blood in her veins turned to liquid fire, and all she wanted to do was stay like this forever. Wrapped in the arms of the man she lov… Christ, there was that 'L' word again.

But all thoughts were lost when he lowered his head and suckled her breast. Arching her back off the ground to press closer, her hands traveled over his shoulders, caressing the smooth, taut skin of his back and landing on his firm arse. Digging her fingers into the solid flesh, urging him to move faster. A fire was building, and she was ready to explode. She couldn't hold back much longer.

Taking the hint, he picked up his pace. Moving eagerly inside her, their eyes locked, and her heart trembled right before bright lights burst behind her eyes. Gasping for breath, she found her release. Nick moaned, low and guttural, a moment after as he found his.

They kissed long and slow as they both came back to earth from their high. When they broke apart, Nick pushed a lock of hair away from her flushed cheek with a gentle finger and brushed a feather-light kiss on her jaw.

And that was when bright lights exploded behind her eyes for the second time. But this time it wasn't due to an earth-shattering orgasm. No, this time it was because, goddammit, she was in love.

<hr>

It was past midnight, and Ava felt ridiculous sneaking into the house. She wasn't a teenager anymore slinking in past curfew. Not that she ever got away with it then. Her dad always busted her every time.

A light flicked on in the study next to the entry, and she blinked a few times to adjust to the sudden burst of light. Her father stood in the doorway, dressed in his robe and slippers.

Busted again.

"It's late. Where have you been?" he asked with a hard tone in his voice.

"I didn't realize I still had a curfew." Ava's shoulders stiffened at being spoken to like a

child.

"You were with Nick, weren't you?" At her silence, he continued. "What were you doing with him this late? No, don't answer that. By the looks of you, up to no good like always." He pointed a finger at her. "Stay away from Nick. He's trouble."

This needed to stop. She was a grown woman with an intelligent mind of her own. She'd already decided that seeing Nick again wasn't a good idea, but she wasn't going to give her father the satisfaction of knowing that.

"Don't you think I'm a little too old for you to tell me what to do?" She started to walk past him to head up the stairs to her room, but he stepped in the way. Boy, he moved fast for someone who was supposed to be sick.

"You'll never be too old, and while you're under my roof I expect you to do as I say."

She threw her head back and laughed, but without humor. "Are you hearing yourself right now?" His only response was a clenched jaw. "Good thing for the both of us I'll be gone in a few days." She stepped around him. "I'll see you in the morning."

"Ava."

She stopped on the bottom step of the staircase but didn't turn around.

"I only want what's best for you. I'm… I shouldn't…" Struggling with the words he wanted to say, he instead said, "Good night."

Her heart squeezed. Many times she'd wanted things to be different between them. Continuing up the stairs, she called back, "Good night." Then she paused and turned around. "Dad."

He stopped at the study doorway. "Yes?"

"If there was something wrong with you, like if you were sick, you'd tell me, right?"

A frown creased his brow. "Of course I would. Why do you ask?"

"Just making sure." She continued up the stairs, relief washing over her.

## Chapter 16

Ava didn't bother knocking when she barged into Bella's room. Although it was just past eleven, it was probably considered the crack of dawn from a teenager's perspective. Bella was on school holiday and apparently wanted to sleep through most of it. But half the day had already passed, and Ava wasn't waiting any longer to find out what her twisted sister was up to.

Throwing back the curtains, drenching the room with golden light, she waited for any sign of life from Bella. The only response was a muffled groan, her head being buried under the

Pooh Bear blanket Ava had bought her when she was five. A smile tugged her lips at seeing Bella still sleeping with it.

"Isabella, wake up!" She pulled back the blanket, and Bella covered her face with her hands like the sun was damaging to her eyes.

Harry wiggled through the blankets and poked his

little white head from out of the covers, not looking pleased about being woken. Yawning, he stretched then sprang from the bed and shuffled out of the room.

"If you don't wake up, I'm going to toss water on you."

"Okay, okay. Geez," she said as she shoved her tangled hair from her face.

Shifting to a sitting position, she leaned back on the headboard and rubbed her eyes. With her hair sticking out around her head and the oversized One Direction t-shirt she wore, Bella could have passed as a ten-year old. Not a teenager with the knowledge—though thankfully not the experience—of sex.

"Tell me the truth. Is Dad sick?" She knew the answer, but she wanted to hear it from Bella. And then she could leave and get back to her life. Well, that was if her car was ready then she could leave.

She needed to put as much distance between her and Nick as possible. The 'L' word still played with her mind. When she woke up this morning she'd hoped it had all been a misunderstanding, caused by the old memories and the romantic setting. No, it pounded in her mind and heart like a drum, and her chest grew warm and fuzzy. It had to stop. Nothing good could come from it.

Fidgeting with the sheet, Bella blinked rapidly. "Y-yes."

"Isabella." She stretched out her name and looked her straight in the eye. "I want the truth."

"I am telling the truth. Why would I lie?" Her tone was defensive.

"I don't know why you'd lie, but I know you are."

Bella opened her mouth to speak, but Ava continued before she could deny it.

"He's showing no symptoms and is looking healthier than ever." And she believed her father when he said he'd tell her if he was sick.

"So? It's too early for symptoms."

Pinching the bridge of her nose, Ava let out a long sigh. "If Dad's really sick, I'm going to make an appointment to see his doctor today."

"No, you can't." Bella's voice cracked and tears sprang from her eyes. Her shoulders sagged, and she dropped her face into her hands.

"Why not?"

"Dad's not sick," Bella admitted.

Ava sighed and sat on the bed next to her. "Then why the story?"

She raised her head, and Ava's heart broke at seeing the pain etched on her sister's face.

"I want us to be a family."

"We are."

She shook her head. "No, we're not. You *never* come home, and when I visit you it's only the two of us."

Guilt sat heavy on her chest. She always knew she should've been around more for Bella but hoped the regular phone calls and her sister coming to visit her would be enough. But as the tears fell from her sister's miserable eyes, she knew she should've put her animosity toward her dad aside for Bella.

"You're right," Ava said, "I've been away too long, but

living here was never easy for me. It's not hard to see that Dad and I don't get along."

"Why don't you?" she asked through waterlogged eyes.

Bella would've been too young to remember the constant arguments or cold shoulders. And she hadn't been born to see how their father had treated Ava's mother. It surprised her that Olivia had stayed with him all these years. These days was he more careful hiding his affairs?

How did she tell Bella their father was a liar and a cheat and crushed Ava's mother's spirit so badly she drowned in alcohol and eventually killed herself? She couldn't. From what she'd seen, Bella had a good relationship with him, and she didn't want to damage that in any way.

"We just clash. I had a lot of teenage angst and rebelled. We never got over our differences." A bit of a weak explanation, but it wasn't the horror story her life had been nor was it a lie.

Nibbling her bottom lip and averting her gaze, Bella said softly, "Mum told me once that Dad and your mum had a bad marriage. She said Dad wasn't very nice to her."

Ava scoffed. "That's putting it kindly." But Bella's wide-eyed expression had her adding, "They had a lot of problems."

"But why do *you* hate him so much? It had nothing to do with you."

"I don't hate him."

"It looks like you do."

"Well, I don't. And I'm sorry I haven't come home to visit. I promise I'll come back again soon." And she would, for Bella's sake. "But you shouldn't have lied about something so serious to get me here."

"You're not going to tell on me, are you?" Her voice was shrill.

Ava narrowed her eyes. "I should. What you did was a terrible thing to do."

"I'm sorry." Bella's eyes once again filled with tears, and her bottom lip trembled.

"You're forgiven. But don't do it again." She pulled her in for a quick hug.

She couldn't tell Bella she wanted to go home as soon as her car was ready, which she hoped was today. If she had to stay an extra couple of days and play happy family, she'd just have to squash down any resentment toward her father, stay away from Nick, and do it for her sister.

Ava entered the dim interior of the stables to visit Amber. The familiar scents of horses and hay that she loved greeted her and tickled her nose. When she reached her horse's stall, she found her father checking Amber's hooves.

"Is she okay?"

Startled, he dropped the hoof pick. Amber whinnied her greeting and stuck her head out of the stall. Brushing her hand over her velvety nose, Ava pulled a carrot from her jean's pocket and gave it to her.

"Everything's fine. I was about to take her out into the paddocks." He slipped a halter over the horse's head, the carrot already finished, and opened the stall's gate.

"Here, let me." Ava held onto the halter, walked Amber outside, and took her to the nearest paddock. She opened the gate and gave the horse a soft tap on the rump.

Securing the paddock, she turned and was surprised to find her father standing behind her. Walking past her, he leaned his arms on the wooden fence. Ava did the same. She should've gone back inside so she didn't have to make uncomfortable small talk, but she loved watching Amber so she stayed.

Amber trotted over to them and rested her head on Ava's shoulder. Laughing, Ava wrapped her arms around her neck.

"She's happy you're back," he said in a gruff tone.

"Why is she even here? You told me you sold her." The long-ago heartbreak resurfaced, and she couldn't conceal the resentment from her tone.

He shrugged his shoulders and, surprisingly to Ava, a moment of sadness crept over his face. "I thought it would make you stay."

"It was a shitty thing to do."

"I know." He didn't even try to make excuses.

"And you've kept her all these years, and you kept my room exactly how I left it. Why?"

"I hoped you'd come home."

Even though Olivia had already told her the same thing, she didn't quite believe it.

A heavy weight dropped to her stomach. She thought he would've been happy not having her around making his life miserable. Because that's what she'd been doing when she'd lived here. She wanted to make his life as miserable as her own. And even though she'd been the biggest brat, he wanted her home. Staying mad at him was getting harder to do.

"I should have made more of an effort," Ava said.

He rubbed a hand over his chin, and the stubble made a scratching sound. A memory of him playfully kissing her cheek when she was little and squealing because it itched sprang to mind. But that was before she was old enough to know her parents' relationship was toxic.

For Bella's sake she was going to force the old hurt down and be part of the family. But there was something she needed to know. "How are you covering up your affairs these days? Olivia looks happy, so you must be getting better at hiding them."

He whipped his head around and glared at her. "What the hell kind of question is that?"

"It's a curious one. You never cared if Mum found out about your affairs, but I'm assuming you're being more discreet now."

Kicking the fence post—which caused Amber to flick her ears back, toss her head, and trot away—he pinned Ava with a hard glare. "I've never cheated on Olivia. Don't start talking crap like that around here. You'll only upset her if she hears you."

"I find it hard to believe you've been faithful all these

years, not after the numerous affairs you flaunted around Mum." The semi-truce that had formed earlier was already crumbling. They couldn't be around each other more than five minutes without getting under each other's skin. "Is that why it would upset Olivia if she heard me? Because she's caught you before?"

"I know you have no reason to believe me after how I treated your mother."

"Pfft, you think?"

"I've never cheated on Olivia. I love her too much to ever do that to her."

"But you didn't give a shit about Mum, so that was okay?" she spat and pivoted on her heels to leave.

Reaching out, he grabbed her by the arm and pulled her back around. "I loved your mother. I fell at her feet like a fool, that's how much I loved her. But things changed…got complicated."

"What changed, what got complicated? All I can ever remember was the hostility between the two of you. You couldn't have been in love for long."

Dark shadows pierced his eyes, and he frowned. "Things didn't work out. We both wanted…needed different things. We made mistakes and hurt each other. We…*I* should have done things differently."

Something big must have happened; she could see the pain in his eyes.

"I'm sorry for what I did, how things…" He cleared his throat. "…ended."

She was too. Sorry she told her mother about her father's mistress, Olivia, being pregnant. Sorry she couldn't stop her from jumping into the car while drunk and killing herself. That was the weight she would live with for the rest of her life. Forgiving her father was more likely than forgiving herself.

---

Nick was washing his greasy hands when a familiar Audi drove into the workshop. He'd seen it many times around town and knew exactly who it belonged to. As he watched Bernardo Cardona get out of the car, he noted that he didn't look like someone who was sick. Then again, his father had looked as healthy as a horse when his heart gave out.

Sauntering over to Nick with an air of arrogance, Bernie trailed his gaze over him like he was sizing him up. It had been years since they'd been in the same room together. The last time hadn't gone too well.

"Come to offer me more money to stay away from your daughter? I didn't need it then, and I definitely don't need it now." Better to get straight to the point. He must know Nick had been seeing Ava; there was no other reason he'd be there.

"Doesn't seem like there's anything I can do about you spending time with Ava. I don't like it, but like she keeps telling me she's a grown woman and can do as she pleases. I figure once she goes back home, you'll quickly be forgotten."

"So, if me seeing Ava isn't a problem, why are you here?" The secret that Bernie had been keeping from Ava sprang to mind. Nick still wasn't sure if she knew, but he had a feeling he was about to find out.

"Oh, you seeing her is a problem. There's just nothing I can do about it. It's what you know that I'm more concerned about."

And there it was. Bernie hadn't told Ava the truth after all these years, and Nick bet Bernie was scared that he was going to let the cat out of the bag.

"Don't you think you should've told Ava by now?"

"No. She's better off not knowing." He waved an impatient hand in the air.

"But she's held onto so much resentment against you all these years. If she only knew the truth about what her mother did…"

"I said no!" Bernie snapped. "It's better to lay all the blame on me than her mother."

Clearing his throat, he pulled his shoulders back. "I trust you'll keep it to yourself?"

At the sight of Bernie's vulnerability, Nick knew it was taking a lot out of him to ask. It must be hard for the big, arrogant son of a bitch, who was used to getting what he wanted, to come and beg for his secret to stay buried.

"I still think it's a mistake keeping this from her."

And Nick didn't like keeping something this huge from her either. Their relationship, although temporary, had shifted after they'd made love last night. He'd yet to call her or she him. Emotions had run high that night, so he figured they both needed some time to sort through them.

If someone had told him that his feelings would have

changed from the anger he'd had toward her only a few days ago, he would've laughed in their face. And now he couldn't stop thinking about her. She occupied every waking moment and starred in some good dreams too. But would he take what they'd started to build any further than the time they had left in Sunland Valley? The answer should be no, but it didn't sit right in his gut...his heart.

"This isn't your business. Make sure you keep the hell out of it," Bernie said, pointing a finger at Nick.

Pretentious, old bastard. Nick nodded stiffly in agreement. It was a family matter, and since Ava was going to be gone soon, this really didn't have anything to do with him.

Bernie nodded back then flicked a glance toward Ava's car. "Is it ready?"

"I just finished it."

"I'll take it back with me and have someone retrieve mine." As he was getting into the car he flung over his shoulder, "Send me the bill." The door closed with resounding force. Then Bernie was gone, and still trying to keep them apart as much as possible.

## Chapter 17

The sun beat down on Nick's shoulders as he nailed the last of the framing around the gazebo. Wiping the sweat off his brow with the back of his forearm, he stood back to inspect his work. It wouldn't be long before the old, run-down structure would be as good as new. Only the floor and a coat of paint was needed, and then it would be back to its original glory.

Seeing the disappointment on Ava's face at how dilapidated it had gotten caused his chest to tighten. It had been a place that held special memories for both of them. He couldn't leave it that way even though his mother was selling the property to Percy. If he'd left it in the state it had been in, Percy was likely to tear it down. During the last two days, Nick had spent hours restoring it so that wouldn't happen.

Over the last two days, Nick had tried calling Ava, but the calls always went to her voice mail. He'd left messages, but she had yet to call him back. Although she did reply to his text message about attending the races and said she'd see him there.

Something deep and more than they both had expected ignited the night they were together on a blanket underneath the stars. Ava dealt with it by avoiding him. He dealt with it by pounding nails and timber together. But now it was time to face what was really happening between them.

He wanted Ava, not only in his bed but in his life. That woman had owned his heart from the day they'd met, and they belonged together. Convincing Ava might not be so easy.

On the day of the races, Ava took particular care in the way she dressed and was pleased with the outfit she'd bought from a cute little boutique in town. She'd spent too much time dressed like a farmer's daughter this past week and not like herself. It was time to glam up. It was like putting her armor back on in preparation to do battle. She was going to need it when she came face-to-face with Nick.

It was also time to leave town. She'd already told Bella she was going back home the day after the races. There was too much work to catch up on, and she couldn't stay any longer. And although her sister was disappointed, she was happy Ava had promised to come back next month and made her lock it in her diary. Ava hoped by then Nick would be back at his *real* work now that Maggie had made the decision to sell, and she wouldn't run into him.

Leaving him tugged painfully at her heart. What she needed to do today wasn't going to be easy, but it was best for them both. Thinking she could keep their time together brief and unattached had been a joke from the beginning. The wall around her heart had crumbled bit by bit from the moment they'd kissed in the pouring rain. And when they made love on the grass, it had crashed into rubble at her feet, leaving her heart open and raw. She couldn't risk being so exposed, because she could get her feelings trampled on again, and she couldn't let that happen.

With one last glimpse in the mirror, she left the room. It was time for Nick to see who she really was and the way she lived her life.

***

The public lawn at the BNW Racecourse was teeming with an array of color. From behind the floor-to-ceiling windows in the VIP lounge, Nick watched men dressed in suits and women dressed in colorful outfits with elaborate headgear, mingling on the grass. Many of the patrons cheered as the magnificent horses thundered on the muddy track toward the finish line.

Others threw their losing tickets on the ground and complained.

It was another great turnout. Trainers from around the country entered their horses in the races BNW Racecourse held four times a year, and thousands of people flocked to the event.

On his left, a loud cheer ripped the air, and he turned to see Bernie getting his back slapped in congratulations from his colleagues. His horse, Winter Sky, had finished first once again. The mare was showing great potential.

But it was the scene outside in the lawn marquee that captured Nick's attention. Amongst the sea of people, he didn't need the bright yellow, figure-hugging dress with the thigh-high split to help find her. Nick could spot Ava anywhere, and he'd bet Ava was down there knowing full well she had a captivated audience. And not just from the men making fools of themselves around her.

Clutching a scotch glass in his clenched fist, he tossed back the amber liquid inside, ignoring the burning sensation in his throat. It didn't compare to the burning in his gut.

She stood surrounded by four admirers who were doing their best to win her attention and no doubt trying to get her somewhere more private. A few times she'd glanced into the grandstand where he was standing right before she plastered a smoldering smile on her face and wrapped an arm around the closest sucker. Because that's what they were—suckers. They were falling for her flirtatious act.

Although the blood in his veins sizzled with heat watching her touch another man, he knew exactly what she was trying to do. This was her way of pushing him away. Too chickenshit to face what was so obviously happening between them.

A curvy woman with dark brown hair slid up beside him and placed a hand on his bicep. But the only dark-haired beauty he wanted feeling him up was the one in the lawn marquee flirting with every man at the racecourse.

"I haven't seen you at Dexter's lately," she purred and pressed up against his side.

Karen, Kylie? He couldn't remember. "I've been busy. Excuse me, I need to be somewhere."

He released her tight grip and stepped away. Her puffy, red lips dropped into a sad pout, but he didn't have time to worry about…Kylie? There was a bigger issue going on below. Ava had chosen her victim and had disappeared around the corner of the grandstand.

Bolting down the stairs, he elbowed through a crowd of punters at the betting ring. Two men tried stopping him to talk, but he ignored them and kept moving. When he arrived at the area he last saw her, it was deserted except for a couple of drunk men sprawled on the ground nursing their beers.

"Did a woman in a yellow dress just come past this way?"

The man who seemed more alert pointed a wobbly hand toward the carpark. "A really hot ch-chick went that w-way with some l-lucky bastard," he slurred.

Fuming even more now, he stormed to the area where the drunk guy had pointed. Was she that scared of facing her feelings that she needed to sabotage their relationship?

Zigzagging through the assortment of vehicles, he finally spotted them. The little prick had her pressed up against a car, his hands heading toward her arse and his mouth at her ear. Red-hot fury blinded Nick. He felt a strong urge to wrap the clenched fists at his sides around the arsehole's neck.

Taking menacing steps toward them, he laid a heavy hand on the guy's shoulder. "Take your fucking hands off her."

***

God, what was Ava doing? These guys who were hanging around like a bad smell were so dull and boring. Only a few months ago conversation, or even mild intelligence, wasn't necessary; a pretty face and a great body was all she'd needed. She'd come to the races to get her old life back, flirt with the cute men, and maybe go a little further with one that took her fancy.

Well aware of a dark, brooding figure standing in the VIP grandstand watching her every move. He needed to see what she was really like and that they had no future together. The sooner Nick understood, the better.

The cute guy with a mop of curly, blond hair was the most attentive, and as soon as some bimbo sidled up and plastered herself against Nick, Ava latched onto the blond's hand and told him she wanted to go somewhere less crowded.

It was all the invitation he needed, and he was off as fast as the racehorses. When they reached what she assumed was his car and he broke out his moves—hands straight on her arse, and slobbering like a happy puppy on her neck—she knew she was kidding herself. She didn't want this. She'd known that as soon as she'd gotten to the races and the men came flocking. But she'd put her plan in motion anyway, hoping to be wrong.

Before she could knock Lassie and his slurping tongue away, the deep tone of Nick's voice cracked around them.

"Take your fucking hands off her."

The curly, blond guy must have had a death wish, because he clung onto Ava's hip and pulled her closer to his side. She wanted to flick him off, but she needed Nick to know this was what she wanted. Sticking to her plan was her only choice. Better for Nick to believe she wasn't someone who could settle for a white picket fence and two-point-five kids.

"She's happy where she is. So why don't you get lost." False bravado peppered the blond guy's words.

"Ava, come with me," Nick demanded.

The anger vibrating from his command was palpable. A chill shot up her spine. "I'm fine where I am," she said.

Nick took an intimidating step closer. Curly, blond guy gasped. The death stare Nick was projecting was enough to scare the bravest of men. "Get your hands off her, and Ava, come with me."

"I'm not yours to control, so back off. I'm not going anywhere with you." Slapping her hands on her hips, she gave him a threatening glare of her own. "Come on." She swung around to take the blond guy elsewhere only to find him stepping away, shaking in his boots. *Crap!* "Umm, I'm gonna go back to the races." And he went scuttling toward the track. Nick's glare had worked.

"Let's go." Nick started to take hold of her hand, but she snatched it out of his reach.

"You can't tell me what to do."

Blowing out a long breath, he pinched the bridge of his nose. "We can do this the easy way or the hard way. It's your choice. Let's go. *Now.*"

"No, Nick. Who do you think you are ordering me around…my father? Not even *he* can tell me what to do, so I'm not going to start listening to you." She shoved past him to go back to the races. Not that she wanted to be there, but anywhere was better than standing in a carpark arguing with Nick.

"It's the hard way then." Pulling her to a stop, he bent at the knees and slung her over his shoulder.

"What the hell are you doing?" she screeched.

"Stopping you from ruining everything."

The gravel under his boots crunched, and all she could see was his arse. Not that it was a bad view, but she was too mad to appreciate it right now.

When she tried to kick her legs to free herself, a shoe fell off. "Stop. I dropped my Manolo Blahnik." But Nick kept moving, the shoulder jabbing into her stomach knocking the breath from her lungs.

"Is there a problem, Mr. Williams?"

Hearing a voice of a potential rescuer, she yelled as loud as she could with the little air she had left in her lungs. "Yes, there is a problem. I'm being detained against my will. *And* he's lost my extremely expensive Manolo Blahnik. Do you know how hard they are to get? So I'm going to kill him."

"No, Riley, there's no problem. Do you mind getting my car?"

"But…the lady said…" There was uncertainty in the man's voice.

"Avi-baby is a little annoyed at being manhandled. Everything's fine."

"Yes, Mr. Williams, I'll get your car."

The sound of scuttling feet eased away, and she assumed he'd done what *Mr. Williams* asked.

"Put me down!" She gritted her teeth and pounded clenched fists against his back. He didn't even flinch at her punches, but dammit, she'd hurt her hand. Of course he had to be built from solid stone, he had a heart to match.

"Stop squirming," he demanded.

The command only made her wriggle and kick more, not caring that her arse was probably exposed to anyone who happened to walk past. She might not be able to break free, but she wasn't going to make it easy for him to hold her.

A heavy hand flattened on her butt. She immediately stilled. Damn, even as mad as she was at him, his palm sent a surge of heat through her body. But she couldn't melt into putty in his hands, so she dropped her head and took a bite of his arse through the black, tailored pants.

Nick yelped. "What the hell?"

"If you don't put me down, I can make things uncomfortable for you too."

A car drove up beside them as Nick was putting her back on her feet. Her movements were jerky as she straightened her clothes. Glancing back from where they came, she spotted the missing shoe, and went to hobble after it only for Nick to put a restraining hold around her wrist.

Through a clenched jaw, she said, "I want my goddamn shoe."

"Riley, can you get the shoe please?" he asked, not taking his eyes off Ava.

"Sure, Mr. Williams."

"We said no other people while we were together." Nick's lips pulled back in a snarl.

"Yeah, well, I changed my mind. I never was good at being monogamous." She threw that at him, hoping he would realize there could never be anything between them.

He shook his head. "Sorry, that wasn't part of the deal."

"Sue me. But I know a few people that will help me out with that. You'd only lose."

"I never lose. So stop fighting and get in the car."

The muscles in her jaw ached from clenching it tightly as she glared at Nick. He opened the passenger side door, gesturing for her to get into a black Porsche—a big step up from his old farmer's truck. She guessed he probably had many more.

Crossing her arms, she refused to do what he wanted.

Sighing, his shoulders slumped. "Just get in the car and stop acting like a two-year-old."

The parking attendant jogged over and hesitantly passed her the shoe. Maybe he was concerned she'd use it as a missile and aim it at Nick's head. The thought was appealing. But she cradled the soft leather in her arms like a baby. She loved it too much to cause it any harm.

"Ava, get in the car or I'll hurl you in." And by the pinched expression on his face, she had no doubt he'd do what he threatened.

A few people had come into the carpark, looking at them curiously, and she didn't want to cause a scene in front of them. With her chin held high, she slid onto the warm leather bucket seat.

Nick climbed in next to her, started the car, and sped out of the racecourse carpark.

While she sat fuming, the town flew by in a blur. She didn't say a word, and neither did Nick. She didn't think he could with his lips pressed so firmly together. *If anyone should be pissed off, it should be me.* They weren't back in the stone ages where men threw their women over their shoulder like their latest kill. And if looks *could* kill, curly, blond guy would've been dead from one blast of Nick's lethal glare. But when he gazed at Ava, it wasn't anger, but disappointment that shot her way. It was for the best; it would make it easier to walk away.

The silence in the air was thick and pressed heavy on her chest. If she was honest, there wasn't going to be anything easy about walking away. But in time, when her heart and head removed the 'L' word, all would be good again in her world. Right? She had to cling onto the belief that it would or she'd crumble. And this time she didn't know how she would pick herself back up.

Soon trees and scrub took the place of buildings, and Ava had no doubt where they were heading. "I'd rather you take me back home." She couldn't be alone with him, because they'd probably end up in bed together, and that wouldn't help her pull away.

Still Nick didn't say a word. Apart from flinging herself out of the car to prevent them from being alone, there wasn't much she could do. Sighing, she nestled back in the soft leather and closed her eyes.

When did dressing up and flirting with good-looking men become so exhausting? Maybe since the shine of her old life started wearing off. And thinking back on the last few months, the glitz and glamour had no longer appealed to her.

The car stopped, and when she opened her eyes, they were already parked in front of Nick's house. The trip went too fast, and the nerves kicked in.

Opening the car door, he got out and walked up the front steps onto the veranda, expecting her to follow. She should stay in the car, but he'd already accused her of acting like a two-year-old, and if she refused to get out, that's exactly how she would be behaving. Pushing the door open, she reluctantly followed him into the house.

"Have you finished playing your games?" His calm tone belied the fierce expression he wore as he stood with hands on hips in the middle of the living room.

"I wasn't playing any games. I was out having fun. The way I live my life."

"Bullshit!" he spat. "You were trying to damage what we have between us, because you're too scared to face what's so damn obvious."

"What's so obvious between us? That we're good in

bed? That's all we have…*had*, nothing more. Whatever we had going on is over. I'm leaving tomorrow."

He barked out a mirthless laugh. "God, Ava, stop fucking lying to yourself." He stepped closer. "Something *is* happening. Own up to it and stop running away."

The words slammed into her like a train. *Running away.* Over the years that was all she'd been doing. Running from her family, from anything that could potentially be a relationship, and running away from Nick.

Would she really have gone with the blond guy if Nick hadn't stopped them? Her heart skidded to a stop at the thought of how it would've hurt him. Christ, he didn't deserve to be treated that way. But he'd seen through her bullshit theatrics.

"It's not that simple," she said quietly. The thought of surrendering to him sent fear rocketing through her veins.

"Yes, it is." The pad of his finger trailed along her jaw. "I want you, Ava, not just for a few days, but in my life forever. And if you weren't too scared to admit it, I know you want me too."

Her heart squeezed as he searched her face with intense blue eyes. A tightness in her throat prevented her from speaking.

"I love you, Ava. I've always loved you."

She sucked in a quick gasp of air. As much as it thrilled her to hear him say those words, the 'L' word sat heavy in her heart, trying to bulldoze its way out. And with Nick staring at her with such emotion, she wished she could say it back.

"This is all too much. I can't think straight." She took a step back and began to pace, pressing her palms on her chest like she was trying to stop her heart from spilling onto the floor.

"Maybe that's your problem. You think too much, you need to let yourself *feel*." He placed his hands on her shoulders, stopping her from wearing a hole in the rug.

She shook her head. "I can't…"

He placed a light kiss on her lips. "Just feel."

And that was the problem—she did feel. How could she not? All the emotions swirling through her body were too much to separate. But the one that screamed the loudest to be heard was the one she couldn't set free.

With her heart pounding, she wrapped her arms around his neck, drawing him down for a kiss. A kiss so deep and so passionate she hoped he could feel what she couldn't yet say. When the kiss broke, she felt him quiver against her.

"Give me time," she said. He opened his mouth to say something, but she quickly added, "Please."

He clenched his jaw and nodded, not looking happy with her decision, but accepting she needed space to sort out her feelings.

"When you're giving yourself time to think, ask yourself one question." He paused and drew in a deep, shuddery breath. "Can you see a life without me? Because I sure as fuck can't see one without you."

With that, he marched out of the house.

# Chapter 18



The next day, Ava went in search of Bella. It was time to say goodbye. She found Olivia in the kitchen. "I've been looking everywhere for Bella. Have you seen her? I'm leaving soon."

"She took one of the horses out for a ride. She won't be long." Olivia wiped her hands on a dish towel. "Would you like a cup of tea while you wait?"

"Sure." She sat down at the table and wished she had time for one last ride.

"It's been wonderful having you back home." Pouring boiling water into two mugs, Olivia carried them to the table and sat down. "Isabella has been so excited having her big sister home, and I haven't seen Bernardo this happy in years."

"I find the part about me being home making Dad happy hard to believe," Ava scoffed.

"You two are both as stubborn and pigheaded as each

other, and too proud to show each other how you're really feeling."

Ava twisted the warm mug in her hand. "We've never had a problem showing each other how we feel."

"No, you say things you don't really mean. Lash out at each other. But what you're *really* feeling is locked away. Bernardo's ashamed of his past and knows he should've handled things differently but hides behind a gruff, overbearing exterior. And you..." Olivia slid a hand across the table to clasp Ava's. "You act defiant and angry, but what you're really feeling is hurt and alone."

Ava pulled her hand away to push shaking fingers through her hair. How did a woman who hardly knew her see through to the core?

"Isabella told me you've promised to visit more often. I'm glad. You and your father have a few wounds to mend."

"Don't get too excited. It might take some time, but he has explained his relationship with my mother. Maybe I can start getting past it now."

Olivia slumped back on the chair with a hand over her heart. "Oh, thank goodness. That secret has been burning a hole in your father's chest for years. He loved your mother. When he caught her having an affair and she told him she was pregnant with her lover's baby, he told me it broke him."

The tea in Ava's stomach churned like acid, threatening to burst out and spill on the table.

All the blood in her body froze to ice as Olivia's words buzzed in her head.

Olivia stopped talking, a stricken expression on her face. "You didn't know all of that, did you?"

Scraping back the chair, it tipped and smashed onto the terracotta tiles. The sound rang out like a gunshot, and Olivia jumped.

"I have to go," Ava choked.

She left with Olivia begging her to stay and calm down, but Ava ignored her pleas.

Turning her back on the sobbing woman, she stormed out of the kitchen.

***

"Were you ever going to tell me you're not my father?"

Bernie was in the on-site vet room talking to Dr. Meyer when she stormed into the room.

Her father's face drained of color, and he asked the vet for a moment of privacy.

When they were alone, he turned to her. "What nonsense are you talking about?"

"Stop lying!" she shouted. "You've been lying my whole damn life. Why didn't you tell me I'm not your daughter?"

Ava never thought her father—or who she thought was her father—looked his age. But now, as he stared at her, he looked every bit of his sixty-eight years. Taking a few steps, he tried reaching out to her, but she stepped back and shook her head.

"Tell me," she demanded.

His arms fell heavy at his sides, and his shoulders hunched. "You *are* my daughter."

"God, enough!" She flung her arms in the air. "I know the truth."

His face screwed up as if he were in pain. "The truth is you *are* my daughter. Look in the mirror, you look exactly like me."

All her life she'd been told she resembled him, she'd even thought so herself. But Olivia said her mother had been pregnant with another man's baby. "Did Mum have an affair?"

He blew out a long breath. "Yes."

"And she told you that the baby—me—wasn't yours?"

He rubbed a hand over his sad eyes. "Yes. But when you were born I knew she'd lied. Not about the affair, but about you. Your eyes were exactly like mine. You can get one of those DNA tests if you need proof. I don't need a test to tell me what I already know."

"All this time I thought you were the one having affairs, but Mum was too?" Christ, how messed up was their marriage?

There was a brown leather lounge in the room and her father sat down, but Ava was too agitated to sit.

Bernie continued, "Your mum only had the one affair...that I know of. To be honest, I drove her to it. I was so busy creating a successful stud farm I forgot I had a wife that needed me at home." Putting his elbows on his knees, he dropped his head into his hands. "She cried and begged for me to be home more often, but I was chasing the money. Then she threatened she'd have an affair because I wasn't paying her enough attention. I didn't believe her and wasn't worried. It was stupid of me to assume she wouldn't. She wanted my attention, and it worked. But I couldn't look at the woman I once loved the same way again. And when she told me she was pregnant with another man's baby to hurt me even more, something inside me snapped and I wanted to break her as much as she broke me."

"Why didn't you just leave?"

"I should have, and many times I wanted to. She could've left too, but no one wanted to take that first step. It was like the love we once had for each other gripped on and wouldn't let go no matter how toxic things became."

"You should have ended it. It ruined Mum, it killed..." Her voice hitched and she couldn't finish.

He dipped his head and stared at his hands. "It killed her, I know. I'm responsible for her death." The anguish lined his face, and her heart bled for the pain it caused.

The anger that had been aimed toward her father all these years started to dissolve as he crumbled from the strain of holding onto the blame of someone's death. She knew exactly how it felt, because she'd been doing the same thing. How many times had she wished that she'd never told her mother about Olivia being pregnant? So many it ate a whole right through her heart until there was nothing left to destroy.

"You weren't responsible for Mum's death, I was." The secret she'd been keeping lifted like concrete from her shoulders. No matter how her father reacted to what she was about to say, she could breathe better for finally setting it free.

His head raised to stare at her. "What are you talking about? You were only a child."

"I found out about Olivia and the baby, and I told Mum. I wanted her to open her eyes and see what you were doing to her. I hoped if she knew about the baby she'd finally leave you and hopefully sort out her life. But after I told her, she freaked out and got into the car."

Shudders ripped through her body, and she wrapped shaky arms around her middle. When her legs no longer had the strength to stand, she dropped on the seat next to her father.

"I begged her not to go. I knew she'd been drinking, but she wouldn't listen. If I had kept my mouth shut, she wouldn't have wrapped her car around a tree."

"God, Ava, none of what happened was your fault. Your mother knew I'd gotten Olivia pregnant. We couldn't keep living the way we were, and I'd already told her I was leaving to be with Olivia. I'd fallen in love, and I had to put an end to our marriage."

She sucked in a shocked breath. "But when I told her she completely lost it. She screamed and cried."

"Probably because *you* found out. She didn't want you to know about the baby. She thought me leaving would've been enough for you to deal with."

If he'd left years earlier, it would've stopped her from seeing the disaster their marriage had been, and maybe Ava wouldn't have had such a twisted view on relationships. But her father was holding onto enough guilt without her adding more. It may have taken many years, but her heart was slowly starting to knit itself back together. And she had Nick to thank for filling the empty space.

She didn't want to hold on to all the resentment she'd been dragging around. It was tiring and emotionally draining. It was time to put the past, and her mother's ghost, to rest.

Reaching out, she held onto her father's hand. It trembled in hers. He swiveled his head around to look at her.

"I'm sorry." And she really was. Sorry for the turbulent family they had, for being such a defiant teenager, and sorry for the distance—not geographically, but emotionally—that she'd put between them.

Tears misted his eyes. "You have nothing to be sorry about. If I could go back in time, I'd change things. I made many mistakes, and I'm ashamed of them. But you…*you* were the light in the darkness. I ruined that too. When you were old enough to understand the tension between your mother and I, you never looked at me the same way again. But please believe me, you *are* my daughter. I've never once doubted it."

"I know. We're both too damn pigheaded to not be related."

They both chuckled.

"I love you, Ava," he said and pulled her into a tight hug. One that was still a little awkward but that could only get better.

"I love you too." The 'L' word wasn't so hard to say after all. It sounded good and felt even better.

When they pulled apart, her father wiped away tears with the back of his shirt sleeve. It was a new experience seeing her strong, tough father so emotional.

"I should be mad at Nick for telling you." His voice was gruff. "But it's a relief that you now know."

*Nick?* His name whirled around her head. "Nick knew about this?" The thin, high-pitched voice was unrecognizable.

"Yes, I thought he told you."

"It was Olivia." And just like that, her heart that had begun to feel whole, collapsed like rubble at her feet.

A painful tightness constricted around Ava's throat, making it hard to breathe. She pulled in air as best she could before she passed out from lack of oxygen. Rising on unsteady legs, she turned to leave.

"Ava, wait." Her father grabbed her wrist. But she pulled free and continued to walk away.

When she reached her room, she locked the door behind her and slid to the floor, dropping her head on her knees. But she didn't let the tears that were building slip out. No, Nick didn't deserve them, nor would she succumb to such weakness.

After the week they'd spent together, how could he have kept something so important from her? And how did he know about it and for how long? She scrubbed her face with her hands. It didn't matter. He'd proved he couldn't be trusted after all. Better to know who he really was now rather than later.

Heaving herself from the floor, she went about packing the few clothes she had, and went to find Bella.

Both Bella and Olivia were in the kitchen, the older woman wringing her hands in distress. Bella was eating a piece of chocolate cake, oblivious to the tension going on around her.

"Ava, is everything okay?" Olivia rushed to her.

"Everything's fine." The smile she put on for Bella's sake felt stiff and brittle on her face.

"I need to head home."

"Aww, already?" Bella wailed.

"Are things good with you and your father?" Olivia gently asked.

"We're okay." A long way from being good, but they'd work on it. Walking over to

Bella, she gave her a hug. "Come visit me during your next holidays."

"You're going to come back here too, right?" she said with pleading eyes.

"Of course."

But first she needed to make sure Nick was long gone. The thought of him sent a sharp jab to her chest. She'd gotten over him once before, and she could do it again. The more she kept telling herself that, the more she would believe it. That was the plan, and she was going to stick to it.

The drive to Maggie's house was quicker than she'd hoped, even though she'd kept under the speed limit. She was in no rush to be on the property. If it weren't for Maggie,

Ava would've been out of Sunland Valley already, but she'd promised her she'd stop and say goodbye.

Also, Lauren had sent Ava an email wanting to buy ten of Maggie's photographs to start with, and if they were popular, like she predicted, she'd buy more. The photo of the dilapidated gazebo was top of the list. It was beautiful, so she could see why Lauren would want it. Ava had planned on buying it herself, but she couldn't stand to look at it anymore.

When she arrived at the house, she let out a pent-up breath, grateful to see neither Nick's truck nor his car parked out front. Hopefully, he was at the workshop and she could say her goodbyes and disappear without crossing paths.

Knocking on the door, she waited a moment for Maggie to answer. The door opened, and the smile Maggie held in greeting slipped when she took one look at Ava. Concern replaced her happy expression.

"What's wrong?" Maggie asked as she ushered Ava inside.

Molly came bounding from the kitchen and danced around Ava's legs. She must've picked up on Ava's mood, because she whimpered, laid down, and rested her head on crossed legs. Ava was good at making everyone upset today. The quicker she got away, the better.

"Nothing's wrong. I've come to say goodbye."

"Come with me," Maggie said, pulling her into the living room and giving her a light

nudge to sit on the couch. "Don't tell me nothing's wrong. I can clearly see there is."

Ava knew there was no point trying to pretend, so she took a deep breath and recapped they day's events.

"And Nick knew about this?" A look of disappointment crossed Maggie's face. Ava nodded. "Surely he must've had a good reason not to say anything."

No matter what his reasons were, it was still a betrayal, and she didn't want to hear any of Maggie's excuses. "I need to go." Reaching over, she gave the woman a quick hug then pulled out Lauren's email from her bag. "Lauren loves your work and has asked me to pass on a list of the photos she wants. All her contact details are there too."

"Thank you. I'm glad she likes them, but please stay a little longer so we can sort this out."

"I can't." The words clogged in her throat. Giving Molly a scratch behind the ears, she then hurried out of the house.

As she approached her car, Nick's truck pulled up beside it. Her stomach dropped. If only she'd left a few minutes earlier, she would've avoided seeing him. Squaring her shoulders for what needed to be done, she waited furiously as he got out of the truck and sauntered over.

A smile that once warmed her from head to toe lit up his face. The sight of him still made her pulse race, but she put it down to the anger boiling in the pit of her gut. Because she wouldn't allow it to be anything else.

He made to hold her around the waist, but she stepped back out of reach. Searching her expression, he said with a serious tone, "Has something happened?"

*Yes, you broke my heart and stomped on it, you stupid jerk* was what she wanted to say, but she wouldn't allow him to know how much of her heart she had given to him. "I know." When he raised a curious eyebrow, she let out a harsh laugh.

"I know about the secret you've been keeping. The one about my *mother*."

His shoulders slumped, and he scrubbed a hand over his face. "You left town before I could tell you."

So, he had known for years. "And what about the past week? You had plenty of time to tell me."

"It wasn't that easy, Ava. God, when you first came back into town we couldn't stand the sight of each other. It wasn't the first thing that came to mind."

"And after that? What about then?" Why did she ever hope she could build a future with him? Her life had been built on secrets, and he had kept them.

"If we weren't ignoring each other or fighting, we couldn't keep our hands off each other. The time was never right." He threw his arms in the air. "Bernie asked me not to say anything. I didn't think it was my business, so I kept quiet. I was wrong. I should have told you. I'm sorry, Ava."

All she could hear was the sound of him tearing out her heart. She swung open the car door. "I don't care what you have to say anymore. It was fun while it lasted."

With that, she slammed the door and turned the ignition with shaky hands. Gravel spat from under the tires as she drove away.

## Chapter 19

"Beth has a hot friend she wants to set you up with." Ben slid a Corona toward Nick as they sat in a booth at Dexter's Pub.

How many beers did this one make? Nick had lost count. Maybe he should stop. His head grew dizzy and two Bens sat in front of him. Fuck it, another one couldn't hurt. Slugging back a mouthful of the cold liquid, he tried to remember what Ben had said. Something about a hot friend.

"She's been eyeing you all night, and Beth reckons she's a guarantee."

Nick glanced in the direction Ben was pointing. A woman with auburn hair wearing a skimpy dress stood next to Beth, smiling and wiggling her fingers at them. Was she hot? He'd seen better. He pictured Ava's face, and he shook it away.

"Come on, boss, she'll make you forget about Ava."

At the sound of her name, a sharp stabbing pain

knifed through his chest. "She did it again. She fuckin' ran away. Why did I fall for her again? Once was bad enough."

"This is why you need to hook-up with Beth's friend. She'll make you forget about Ava." "Stop saying her name." He groaned like he was in pain.

"Sorry, boss. Look, they're coming over. Act nice and give her a chance."

The two women strutted over and slid into the booth. Beth next to Ben and auburn-haired woman friend next to Nick.

Beth made the introduction. "Nick, this is Lucinda. Lucinda, this is Nick."

Lucinda slid closer to him so they were touching from shoulder to knee. Twisting in her seat to say hi, her generous breasts pressed against his chest. The hand she placed on his thigh wasn't shy. Her palm slid seductive and slow toward his lap.

Maybe this *was* the best way to forget about Av… Now he couldn't even think her name. Looking over at Ben, his mate gave him a thumbs-up sign and wiggled his eyebrows.

Sliding an arm across the back of the booth, Lucinda snuggled in even closer. Any closer and she'd be giving him a lap dance.

Nuzzling at her ear, he whispered, "Want to get out of here?"

When Nick woke the next morning, the sun beamed so bright into the room he threw an arm over his eyes to block out the harsh rays. A fierce pounding split his brain. Groaning, he sat on the edge of the bed, hung his head between his knees, and waited for the room to stop spinning. He took a few deep breaths through his nose to settle the rolling queasiness in his gut.

God, how much did he have to drink last night? Ben kept sliding them over to him, and he kept putting them away. Beers weren't the only thing he remembered. A hand on his thigh, a breast against his chest, and red auburn hair in his face.

Whipping his head around—which wasn't the smartest thing to do because pain exploded behind his eyes—he glanced at the bed with dread. When the other side was empty, he sagged with relief. Parts of the night flittered blurrily through his mind. He thought he could erase one woman with another. But Ava wasn't easy to forget.

Getting off the bed, he walked to the bathroom and had a hot shower. The next thing he needed was coffee. The stronger the better.

He got dressed then headed to the kitchen. Fifteen minutes, and two cups of coffee later, the fog in his mind cleared and he could once again think straight. After asking Lucinda to leave the bar with him, he'd changed his mind as soon as his arse heaved from the seat. The look on her face when he told her he was going home alone was comical, part shocked and part death stare. Ben tried unsuccessfully to get him to stay. Once out of the bar, he'd gotten a lift home from a mate and fell into a coma-like sleep.

And now fully conscious, all thoughts turned back to Ava. No matter how much he tried or how much alcohol was consumed, he couldn't get her out of his head. She'd gone and left him *again*. And if he hadn't showed up when he did, she would've left without a word. Running away was what she was good at. Running away from anything that got too tough. Well, it was time he moved on too. There wasn't more he could do in Sunland Valley; there hadn't been for a long time.

When Nick walked into his mother's house, he found her removing frames from the walls. "Packing to leave so soon?" he asked as he reached over her to remove a photo hung higher on the wall.

"No, just doing a few things so it's not so much later." He could see the excitement at moving in her eyes, but knew she was trying to tone down her enthusiasm for his sake.

"I was going to go back to Sydney today, but if you need me to help…"

"No, no." She waved the offer away. "I'll be fine. I've arranged a removalist. You need to get back to doing *your* job."

"Sounds like you're ready to get rid of me."

Cupping his face in her hands, she pulled him down

to kiss his cheek. "I never want to get rid of you, but you need to live your life, not your father's."

Clenching his jaw, he nodded. The feeling that he was letting his father down was still simmering in his heart.

"*And*," his mother continued, "you need to fix things with Ava."

"There's nothing to fix. She made her choice," he said, calm and quiet, surprising himself with his restraint. Inside he wanted to punch a hole in the wall.

"The two of you are as stubborn as each other. You kept a secret from her, a *huge* secret, and it hurt her."

"She didn't listen to my explanation."

"The way she sees it, you had plenty of opportunities to explain."

He never thought their relationship would get to the point where they shared that kind of stuff. And it was her father's secret, not his.

"Life isn't always easy. What if something else makes her take off? I can't keep chasing her when she runs."

"When have you ever?" his mother gently pointed out, but to Nick it came across as subtle as a brick to the head. "You love her, Nicky. I know you do. Go stop her from running."

"She made her choice." He pecked his mother on the cheek. "I'll come back as soon as I can to help with the move." With that, he left the house and the farm he grew up on.

## Chapter 20

The factory was ready for the grand opening. The buzz of excitement from the showroom downstairs reached Nick as he sat in his office. This should've been the most exciting day of his life, but instead, he wanted to be anywhere but here.

The last couple of weeks he'd overseen all the hard work Brad had put into the factory. Something Nick should've done beside him. But now Nick was the one who got to do the opening because Brad's wife Lexi gave birth to a beautiful girl three days ago.

Nick had called Brad to keep him up to date on the progress, but the birth of his daughter outshone the birth of the factory, and he only wanted to talk about how great Lily's burp sounds were. When Nick Facetimed Brad, he couldn't miss the dark smudges under his brother's sleep-deprived eyes. He probably hadn't slept in the three days she'd been born, but the smile on his face and the sparkle in his eyes showed he loved every minute with his new baby girl.

If things hadn't gone to shit with Ava, could they have one day shared the same experience? Would he be looking at the little face of a girl who had her mother's eyes? He shook his head to remove the image. No point thinking about something he'd never have with Ava.

She'd made herself perfectly clear—things were over.

A knock sounded at the door and Gia, his assistant, poked her head around it to announce they were ready to start.

"I'll be right down."

She smiled, then left.

He heaved himself off the chair, removed his suit jacket from the back of the seat and put it on, then tugged his tie and made his way downstairs to face the media storm.

A ribbon was cut and cameras flashed. Dozens of questions were thrown Nick's way, but he couldn't remember any of them. He only hoped his answers corresponded with the questions.

After the formalities were done, it was time to open the champagne, and waiters passed it out generously to the guests. He smiled and shook hands until he thought his face would crack. The atmosphere was electric, but he couldn't plug into it, and a headache pounded at the back of his eyes. Would anyone notice if he slipped out quietly?

Who cared if they did? He'd had enough of pretending he was happy. It was time to leave. When he decided to make his move and head toward the nearest exit, a heavy hand landed on his shoulder. Annoyed that his getaway had been stopped, he sighed and turned to meet the laughing expression of Robin Parry, the CEO of a major car company.

"You managed to pull off a great launch. But I'll be more impressed if I see that you can actually sell anything as good as what we have." Robin snagged two champagne flutes from a passing waiter and handed one to Nick.

"You better be careful, we'll be coming after you. You *should* be worried." Nick raised the glass in a salute.

Robin chuckled. "Ahh, Nick, always chasing the dream. I admire that, but will you get there? I don't know."

*Always chasing the dream.* When it came to business, he chased until he got exactly what he wanted. It all started when he wanted to own the workshop in Sunland Valley. But that hadn't been enough. He'd chased the dream of turning it into a caryard and having them in all major cities. He'd chased the dream of opening up a factory to make his own cars.

The conversation he had with his mother before he left replayed in his mind.

*"I can't keep chasing after her when she runs."*

*"When have you ever?"*

And that's exactly what he let Ava do. He let her run off ten years ago without a fight. He never followed her demanding an explanation, instead choosing to believe the lie surrounding them. It had been easier to believe the deceit than believe in what they had. And like an idiot, he let her go again. If there was anything more important and worth chasing, it was Ava. He could have all the success and money in the world, but it didn't mean shit if he didn't have Ava in his life.

His marriage to Kate never worked because he could never love her. Never love her because Ava had always filled his heart. And he knew without a doubt that a future with her was all he wanted. It had always been Ava and always would be. She was worth the chase.

Handing over his untouched champagne to Robin, he excused himself. "I've gotta go. I have an even bigger dream to chase."

Ava glanced at the clock and willed for the time to pass quickly. Mrs. Johnston had spent the past half hour bitching about her two-timing, soon-to-be ex-husband and his new perky-tits girlfriend.

"I want to take everything he's got. I'm not leaving a thing for her to sink her acrylic claws into."

"Mrs. Johnston, we've already discussed how you're dividing the assets. You were content with the decision."

"Well, that was before I found out about miss perky-tits." Crossing her arms over her heaving chest, she tilted her chin. "Now you can rip up those documents and start again."

Blowing out a long, frustrated breath, Ava pinched

the bridge of her nose. Thank God she never had to personally deal with this in her life.

Glancing out the window, she could see the Williams caryard sign in the distance. Funny how for years she'd sat in this office and never noticed it before. Now it stood out like a neon light flashing in her eyes. Reminding her of Nick's betrayal and how she was struggling to claw out of the dark pit she'd plunged into.

"And if she thinks she's going to live in the house that *I* paid for, she can think again."

Ava had zoned out, drawn into her own thoughts, and only heard the last of her client's ranting.

"I'm sorry, Mrs. Johnston, but I have another appointment. We'll have to continue this another time." She stood, walked over to the door, and opened it, giving the woman no other choice but to leave.

When Mrs. Johnston left, she heaved a sigh of relief. There wasn't another appointment, but she couldn't listen to the whinging woman a moment longer.

Walking over to the window, she stared at the sign, and her heart trembled behind her ribs. As much as she tried to squash thoughts of Nick from her mind, they were always front and center. She went to sleep thinking about him, dreamed of him, and woke up craving him. She'd hoped she'd only imagined falling in love. That it had all been caused by old memories and good times flooding back. But she couldn't deny the feelings were real...strong. And that was why it hurt so damn much.

*"Ask yourself one question. Can you see a life without me?"* The words echoed in her mind. The emptiness of not

having him in her life consumed her and spread like a disease through her body. She was waiting for it to pass with time. This couldn't last forever, could it?

Like she always did when thoughts of Nick entered her mind, she threw herself into work, but after reading and re-reading Mrs. Johnstone's divorce papers and not coming up with any solutions on how to adjust them—because she wasn't starting again; she'd spent hours negotiating to get it to this point—Ava decided to put it away and deal with it tomorrow. In fact, all her cases could wait until the next day. She was too tired to do any more and would probably make things worse. With that thought in mind, she left the office.

Walking to work this morning had seemed like a good idea. The sun had warmed her skin, and she could use a bit of vitamin D. She'd been cooped up at home or in the office for a month. The fresh air and sunshine would do her good. If only she'd checked the afternoon weather forecast. A storm had been predicted, and it happened to hit while she was only a few meters from home. Having no umbrella, the deluge of water soaked through to her skin. And when she thought things couldn't get worse, a truck flew past, spraying her with muddy gutter water.

Finally arriving at her front door and under shelter, she found two parcels wrapped in white paper leaning against the wall next to the door. One was labeled *open first*. The other labeled *open second*. There was no postage on them, so someone must have hand-delivered them.

Unlocking the door, she picked up the square objects and took them inside. She was a little apprehensive about bringing something into her home when she didn't know where it came from, but curiosity about what was inside won. It didn't look too sinister. They were about sixty centimeters high and wide, and if she had to guess she'd say they were photo frames. Did Maggie drop off some photos? But why would she drop them off without telling her or leaving a note?

Not able to wait any longer, Ava kneeled and tore into the paper labeled *open first* and gasped. Covering her mouth, she leaned back on her heels. It was the black-and-white photograph of the gazebo that had been hanging on Maggie's wall. The one that she had loved despite the fact that the sight of the destruction made her heart ache. Hot tears burned behind her eyes, but she held them back. When she opened the next parcel, she did it slower and with more care. Her hands shook as she pulled back the paper.

The gazebo that was once ready to be pulled down was now restored. The colored photo displayed a bright white structure standing strong and proud amongst a background of green foliage. A colorful array of daises bordered the edges, and baskets filled with yellow begonia hung from the beams. It was beautiful, even more so than what she remembered.

Nick did this, she knew it. No one would have bothered repairing something that was ready to crumble. Something no one used anymore. But the gazebo was her special place; a place she could go to and block out the world. Nick knew how much it meant to her, and he brought it back to life.

The years of suppressing all her pain, fears, and sorrow came flooding out. The sobs she'd never let come out since her mother's death ripped through her body, and tears fell like hot rain down her face. She sat on the floor crying for the loss of her mother, crying for the distance between her father, but mostly crying for the love she threw away with Nick. All because she let her insecurities destroy her trust in men. And at the first sign of trouble she ran away. Ran away from the only man she ever wanted to hand over her heart to and build a life with.

A tiny part of her wanted him to come after her. Hell, a big, fat chunk of her wanted him to fight for her. But why would he? In the last conversation they had he'd tried to explain why he'd kept her father's secret, but she wouldn't listen. All she could hear was another man letting her down. But she'd let Nick down by blaming him for keeping her father's secret, and that wasn't fair.

God, she'd let go of the only man she'd ever opened her heart to, the one man she'd *always* loved. All these years she'd blamed her promiscuous father for her unhealthy relationships with men, and yes, it had played a big part. But it was losing Nick the first time that really caused her to close her heart and build a solid brick wall around it, giving no other man any chance. Because there could be no other man.

*"Ask yourself one question. Can you see a life without me?"* Hell no, she was only fooling herself into believing she could.

The urge to go to him pulled her up onto her feet. She

needed to tell him she loved him, and she prayed his feelings hadn't changed.

Then she remembered he was in Singapore opening up the Williams factory. Well, if she was going to declare her love, she might as well make it good. So, if that meant flying to another country, that's exactly what she'd do.

A knock sounded at the door just as she was about to book the next available flight to Singapore. She didn't have time to waste on visitors. Whoever it was, had to go.

Before she opened the door, she glanced at her reflection in a mirror next to it and gasped with horror. Thanks to the rain and the truck splashing filthy gutter water over her, her hair hung in tangled clumps and her clothes were damp and dirty. The crying episode gave her blotchy cheeks, and mascara streaked down her face, giving her Alice Cooper eyes. She tried wiping the black smudges off her face but only made it worse, and the eyes staring back at her were puffy and red.

The knock pounded again. Oh well, she looked like a wreck, there was nothing she could do about it now, and she opened the door.

Standing on the veranda, with clothes rumpled and bloodshot, tired eyes, was Nick. Her heart trembled, and her knees shook. Not sure if she really was seeing him through swollen eyes, she blinked rapidly, but he still stood in her doorway. God, she'd missed him.

"Can I come in?" he asked softly.

A moment ago, she was ready to jump on a plane to pour her heart out, and now having him here only inches away, scared her to death. What if she couldn't say what she really wanted to? What if she could but he didn't want to hear it? He was here, at her home, surely that was a good sign? But his mouth was unsmiling and she couldn't read anything in his clear blue eyes.

"Can I come in?" he asked again.

Moving aside, her hand shook as she gestured him inside.

His gaze explored her face, and a frown creased his brow. "Have you been crying?" "Allergies," she lied. It killed her for him to see the mess she was in.

He cocked an eyebrow, and his full lips pulled into a flat line. Lips she was desperate to kiss. "Why were you crying?" Of course he didn't believe her lame excuse.

"Because…because…I love you, you big idiot. You send me the most gorgeous photos. And they made me cry like a baby, and now I look like crap. And if you don't love me back, then you better leave right now, because I will *not* fall apart in front of you." Too late…tears streamed from her eyes, and her body trembled.

This was not the way she planned to profess her love. In her mind she was wearing the sexy, black Valentino dress she'd bought two months ago, hair and makeup was on point, and she'd articulate her feelings in a well-presented manner. Not the garbled bunch of words that spewed out of her mouth from someone who looked like a chaotic lunatic.

Nick dug his hands in the pockets of his well-worn, faded jeans and glanced over at the

photos she'd left on the floor. "You think I sent them?"

Sucking a quick breath, she covered her face and groaned into her hands. *God, I'm such a fool.* "You didn't?"

"I did." Stepping closer, he took her hands away, grinning with a sparkle of mischief in his eyes.

"What? Oh, you're such an arse!" She made to push past him, but he clutched both her wrists and tugged her to him, pressing their chests together. The vibration of his heart pounded against her.

"I *am* an arse, for letting the best thing in my life walk away from me. Not once, but twice." Pain clouded his eyes. "I know I don't deserve you. I should never have kept that secret from you. I'm sorry. If I could change things, I would. But to hear you tell me you love me…" He dropped his forehead onto hers and drew in a shaky breath. "Makes me the happiest man alive. I love you, Ava. I always have and always will. You're all I want."

A lump formed in her throat, making it difficult to talk, and the damn tears leaked again.

So instead of speaking, she pulled his head down for a kiss that promised love and forever.

When they broke apart Ava's voice wavered. "I asked myself the question. I *can't* see a life without you. I love you, Nick. I should never have blamed you for something that was my father's fault."

"Let's put that behind us, but promise me one thing. No more running?" He dipped his head to stare into her eyes. "If you do, I'll only keeping chasing after you."

"No more running. You're stuck with me through the good and the bad." She glanced down at her wet and muddy clothes. "And this is kinda bad."

He laughed and pulled her in tighter. She would never tire of his strong, firm body against hers.

"I'll just have to put up with it," he joked. "You can be covered in mud or cow shit and

I'll still love you."

"Aww, now there's a man who understands how to romance a woman."

"You better believe it, Avi-baby. That's only the beginning."

## Epilogue
### ONE YEAR LATER

*F*airy lights twinkled as they hung from the branches of the surrounding trees, competing for attention with the stars displayed in the ebony night sky. A soft breeze with a hint of Magnolia blossoms scented the air. The tables scattered on the grass were filled with food and drink and surrounded by their family and friends.

Wrapped in Nick's arms, Ava swayed in time to the string quartet set up inside the gazebo where earlier Nick and Ava were announced husband and wife in front of all the people they loved. It was the best agreement she'd ever made.

"You seem a little quiet, Mrs. Williams." Nick gazed at her.

Would she ever tire of looking at that gorgeous face? She didn't think so. Today his dark hair had been trimmed for the wedding, but she'd always love the unkempt farmer boy style.

"Who said I was changing my name? You already convinced me not to sign a pre-nup." She had to admit she was pleased he didn't want anything to do with one. And she didn't even feel sick about it. They were in this forever; she wouldn't accept anything less. "How about Mrs. Cardona-Williams?" she offered.

"As long as that ring stays on your finger, I don't care what you call yourself." Lowering his head, he kissed her softly. She quivered. "What are the chances of getting rid of everyone so we can christen this gazebo as husband and wife?"

Glancing around the grassy clearing where a wedding marquee had been set up, she watched her family and friends celebrating and couldn't see anyone leaving anytime soon. "They don't look like they're going anywhere. We can always come back tomorrow and spend the whole day here."

Ava laughed at the disappointed expression on Nick's face. Because she couldn't wait a moment longer to be alone with her husband. *Husband!* She never thought in a hundred years she'd call a man her husband, and she loved the sound of it.

She suggested, "Your ute's not parked too far away. If we're quiet, we might be able to sneak—"

Without letting her finish, he grabbed her hand and they ran down the gazebo's steps.

"Let's go!"

Read on for a sneak peek into
Lauren and Jack's story The Trouble with Mr. Pretty

<hr>

# The Trouble With Mr Pretty
## CHAPTER 1

<hr>

*L*auren Moore swung the *closed* sign of her gift shop into place and glanced through the tinted glass. The street had been blocked, stopping vehicle access to the quaint shops in the seaside village, and now the street was beginning to fill up with rowdy people ready to celebrate the New Year. She smiled and made her way to the back of the shop, thankful she'd be gone before the crowds rolled in.

Post-Christmas trading had been the busiest in years, and Lauren had rung up the sale for the last customer only moments ago. Her legs ached from standing all day, and a headache pounded at her temples. She couldn't wait to go home, soak in the tub, then crawl into bed. She longed for the oblivion of sleep to block the memories of the worst New Year's Eve of her life. She didn't want to remember that night; the pain always brutally crushed her heart.

Thunderous banging sounded behind her. Startled,

she swung around. A tall, silhouetted figure stood on the opposite side of the dark glass. Taking a few steps closer, she pointed at the sign.

The knocking grew louder and more persistent, then the man put his hands under his chin as if in prayer and mouthed *please*.

Feeling drained from the day, she sighed, slumped her shoulders, and pulled the keys out of her pocket. Then she made her way to the door and opened it. Would this day ever end?

On a gust of December heat the man barreled into her shop of dainty gifts, and did a quick scan of the area before stopping in front of a display of delicate tea sets. With his broad shoulders and chest, he looked too big to be anywhere near her pretty breakables. She needed to get him out fast.

"Is there something I can help you with?" She asked, her attention focused on the expensive teapot in his large, strong hands.

She breathed a sigh of relief when he set the fragile item back on the shelf before turning to face her. "You're a lifesaver for opening for me."

His crooked smile flashed white teeth and the force hit her like a lightning bolt to the chest. She drew in a sharp breath as heat rushed through her veins. The greenest eyes she'd ever seen surrounded by thick, dark eyelashes sparkled at her while faint creases fanned out from the corners. His dark brown hair was cut short at the sides of his head but kept longer on top. It looked tousled, like impatient fingers had ploughed through it. His faded denim jeans, stamped with a designer label, molded firmly around a tight rear end and muscular legs, something she'd gotten a brief glance at before he turned. A black shirt stretched across his broad shoulders, the top buttons open, giving her a peek of a strong chest.

The man was absolutely gorgeous, and the fact she noticed was shocking. Her best friends, Ava and Jade, often teased that if Channing Tatum walked past she wouldn't give him a second glance because Lauren no longer saw a pretty face...well, up until now. This man, and the pretty packaging he came in, couldn't be ignored, and she wondered why out of all the men who, according to her friends, were babes, did she notice this one? He looked vaguely familiar. She couldn't put her finger on where she might have seen him before, but she was positive he'd never been a customer.

Ava and Jade would freak if she told them she'd finally noticed a *Mr. Pretty*. Actually, keeping this unsettling discovery to herself was best. They'd start setting her up on blind dates again with all the pretty boys they knew. No, she couldn't put herself through that torture again. Those dates had been disastrous. They'd been good-looking men who couldn't see past their own attractive reflection. Although a part of her felt relieved that after all these years she'd finally noticed a handsome man; she wasn't broken after all...well, not completely.

"I need something to get myself out of big trouble," he finally answered. His deep voice sounded as smooth as whiskey.

Heat sizzled and stirred around her, making the room

feel like a sauna. Was the air conditioning off already? The need to get him out of the shop fast was crucial; otherwise, she feared she might melt into a steamy puddle at his feet.

"Does 'getting you out of *big* trouble' have a price tag?" she asked.

"After the mess I'm in, the sky's the limit." He grinned.

"A desperate man with lots to spend—you're my favorite customer," she joked, keeping it light while her insides turned to quivering mush. "How much trouble are you in?"

One large shoulder shrugged as he dipped his head and dug his hands into the pockets of his jeans. "Enough for me to pound on your door after closing time."

The devilish smile showed he knew how to get himself out of all sorts of trouble. Why did men think women could be appeased by a charming smile and expensive gifts? A stab of shame pierced Lauren's thoughts as she remembered a time when she could be won over by sparkly trinkets and a dazzling smile. She'd learned the hard way that shiny things soon tarnished.

She led him to a black velvet display. "We have beautiful lockets with intricate designs and some with lovely colored gems. What's your wife's style?"

"I'm not married."

"Your girlfriend?"

"It's for my mother," he clarified.

"Oh." She hadn't seen that coming. A get-out-of-trouble gift was usually for a lover.

Her friends had to constantly remind her that not all handsome men were scheming jerks with secret agendas, but she had yet to meet one. After her horrifying experience with Graham Stone, she never wanted to look at, or get involved with, another good-looking male ever again.

With stiff fingers, she touched the locket around her neck. It wasn't one of the pretty gem-encrusted ones she sold, but to her it was much more valuable. Lauren had found the cheap silver locket years ago at a small seaside market she'd been aimlessly walking through. A precious yet painful reminder lay locked inside. A big reminder of why she kept away from men who looked too good to be true.

Needing to focus on work, Lauren inwardly shook herself. Scanning the shop, she decided a vase might be more appropriate for his mother and moved closer to a display cabinet with a colorful array of crystals in all shapes and sizes.

"These are lovely if you think your mother would like them."

He ambled over to the cabinet, closing the distance between them. The smell of sunshine, sea breeze, and man surrounded her and sent her senses into overdrive. She clutched anxious fingers around her locket and stepped away, only for her back to press against the wall, giving her no more room to move.

As he looked inside the cabinet, oblivious to the turmoil he was causing her, Lauren examined his profile. The start of an afternoon shadow covered a square jawline. His long, narrow nose had a small bump on the bridge, the only flaw on his chiseled face. He bit his lower lip as he studied the vases, and for a moment, she wondered how they would taste.

Where were these outrageous thoughts coming from?

Lauren desperately needed to put more space between them. Standing so close was making it impossible to think, but to move would involve brushing past him. Touching him wasn't going to help with her jumbled thoughts and sensations. She hadn't reacted to a man like this since Graham.

When she trusted her voice not to quiver, she excused herself. He stepped back, giving her room to pass, but not enough to avoid contact, and her bare arm brushed the length of his strong, firm one. Another blast of heat shot from him and into her. Blinking up at him, their gazes locked, and she searched those piercing green orbs to see if he'd felt it too. His emerald eyes held hers.

Unable to pull away from his penetrating gaze, she reached for the metal locket, but its coolness did nothing to remind her that being so close to this heat-missile was a bad idea.

A shrill tooting of horns outside the shop broke the spell, and she glanced out the window. A bunch of excited New Year's Eve revelers, with colorful hats and party horns, crowded the footpath in front of the shop.

"They've started early," she said on a shaky breath, using the noisy distraction to move away from him. She scurried behind the counter, putting a safety barrier between them.

He flicked a glance over his shoulder at the partygoers. "It will be a great night for it."

By his casual stance she would have believed him unaffected by the burning moment they'd just shared, but heat still smoldered in his eyes. Then, in a blink of an eye, it was gone. Could she have imagined it? It had been so long since anyone had come even close to looking at her that way that she probably read the signs wrong.

Needing to get back to the reason he was there, and not be distracted by that liquid green heat, she cleared her throat. "Do you see anything you like?" She relaxed a little because her voice sounded professional and not like the trembling mess simmering on the inside.

The liquid heat was back in his eyes and they raked over her in a way that said *she* was what he liked. A sharp breath caught in her lungs and her heart began to race. Surely she didn't get *that* signal wrong?

"The vases…do you like any of them?" she managed to croak out.

His lips tilted in a knowing smile, like he knew she'd been rattled, then he sauntered closer, as if he had all the time in the world. "They're very nice, but her house is full of them. I recognize a couple in your display."

*God, hurry up and pick something, then leave!* The warm, relaxing bubble bath she planned for the evening would have to be replaced with a long, cold shower. "Do you have any idea what her tastes are?"

"I do know she loves this shop. She tells me she comes here all the time. I think she's dropping hints for me to buy stuff from here."

"Looks like it worked. What's your mother's name? If she's a regular customer, I'd probably know who she is."

"Susan Henderson. I'm Jack." He stood there with his hand out.

The name froze her on the spot for a beat. Now she knew why he looked so familiar, but it wasn't because of a family resemblance to his mother. It was because Jade had been drooling over the man standing in Lauren's shop for over a decade. Until a couple of years ago, Jack had been the captain of Jade's favorite football team, The Flaming Stars. He was now retired due to an injury. Susan often spoke of her children but never mentioned she was the mother of a very famous football player. Lauren, who wasn't into sports or sport stars, never knew the two were related.

Jade also followed Jack off the football field and kept Lauren and Ava updated on his social life. Lauren refused to read gossip magazines since the day she had seen Graham's proud, beaming face staring back at her from the pages of one of them with the news that had shocked her life. But Jade loved reading them, and according to her, Jack had been involved with a string of women from actresses to supermodels and everything in between. Lauren always believed Jade exaggerated his infamous relationships. The media liked to embellish or even make stories up so they could sell their magazines. But after seeing Jack in the flesh and witnessing his charm, she could understand how women didn't stand a chance against him.

From the moment he charged into the shop he

embodied confidence, charm, and beauty. His casual clothing did nothing to hide the quality and expense, nor did they hide the powerful body beneath them. Instincts screamed to keep her distance. Jack was definitely a *Mr. Pretty*. Mr. Pretty was a nickname Jade and Ava had made up when Lauren started keeping away from all attractive men, especially if they were also very successful.

Warning bells clanged *back away now*! If he weren't Susan's son, she would have quickly ushered him out the door, with or without a gift. But Susan was one of her best customers and someone whom she liked very much. Not only did Susan shop there often, she'd noticed Lauren's unique way of decorating the place and encouraged—more like insisted—Lauren redecorate Susan's bedroom. The woman had been so happy with the results she passed on a good word to her friends. With another two bedrooms lined up for clients, Lauren was busy collecting the necessary pieces. It was very exciting that her business was branching out into design. A little scary too. She wasn't a qualified interior designer but people were trusting her with their homes.

Eyeing Jack's waiting hand like it was a snake ready to strike, she reluctantly accepted it. His large, firm grip smothered hers, and a jolt of heat zapped up her arm to slam into her chest.

Freezing for a beat, she finally managed to say, "I'm Lauren Moore. Susan told me about her inconsiderate son not making it home for Christmas. I assume this is why you're in her bad books?" She tried to sound amused.

"She's made no secret that she's not happy with me."

He chuckled, keeping her hand in his strong grasp and showing no signs of letting go. Heat traveled at the speed of light through the rest of her body, warming her from head to toe.

The warning bells clanged louder, telling her to move slowly and carefully away from the imminent threat. With a light tug, she pulled her hand free and placed it on the counter's surface, hoping the cool stone would help bring her body temperature back to normal. It didn't work.

*Focus.* Lauren needed to focus, sell him something, and get him to leave. She didn't understand what the reaction to him was about. This was new to her. "I have a mirror in my office I put aside for her because she was looking for something to hang in her entryway. I'm sure she'll love it. Just give me a minute and I'll get it."

She hurried to the office, thankful for a few minutes alone to get her messed-up head and body back in order. Closing the door behind her, Lauren leaned back on it, shut her eyes, and took a deep breath. It helped with her shaking hands but did nothing to slow her racing heart.

There wasn't anything she could do about her heart rate so she picked up the French provincial style mirror leaning against the wall and glanced at her reflection. Bright pink spots flushed her cheeks and neck—the result of a mere brush of an arm and a touch of a hand. What was happening to her?

When her body settled down, allowing her to function normally, Lauren carried the mirror into the shop and placed it on the counter. "If Susan doesn't love it, she can always bring it back and exchange it for something else."

Jack flipped over the little white tag, revealing the price, and whistled. "My mother sure does have expensive taste."

Guilt gnawed at her for showing him such an expensive item. "I have candlesticks which are much cheaper, and I'm sure she'd like those too."

She started to pick the mirror up to take it back to her office, but he placed a hand on it, stopping her. "If I want to get back into her good books, I better make it great."

"Having you home will be enough for Susan. She doesn't need gifts."

"How she has you fooled." He chuckled.

His smooth laugh sent a shiver up and down her spine. Damn, she needed to get him out of the shop. The sooner the better.

Lauren carefully placed the mirror in a box, wrapped it up in pretty pink and white paper, and attached an elaborate pale blue bow in the corner. After ringing up the sale, she wished him luck with his mother and led him to the door.

"Thanks for opening for me." He held out his hand, and she had no other choice but to take it. A quick, feather-light stroke of his thumb brushing along her fingers had Lauren sucking in a soft gasp. *Did his eyes just drop to my lips?*

She let go of his hand as if burned by hot coals and leaned past him to open the door, making every effort for their bodies not to touch.

He stepped onto the street filling up with partygoers and said, "Happy New Year, Lauren."

"Happy New Year, Jack." She quickly averted her gaze and closed the door with a resounding *click*.

Turning her back toward the man that had barreled into her shop and upset her senses, Lauren walked over to turn the lights off, but before she did, she took a moment to glance around the room. She was proud of her shop—Everything Nice—with its mixture of what she believed to be beautiful and feminine. She stocked everything from unique and unusual homewares, pictures, tea sets, and clocks to more personal items such as jewelry, perfumes, and lingerie.

Lauren began working at Everything Nice when she started university, then, two years ago, she bought the business from her boss and wonderful friend Lillian. When Lauren took over, it only needed a fresh coat of paint and a revamp of the tired-looking sign on the front window. Now, with Lauren's name on the paperwork, the responsibility of keeping it successful lay on her shoulders.

Lauren never thought she'd be a shop owner. She'd spent her first year at university studying to be a lawyer. Her job at Everything Nice was only meant to be tempo-rary; something to help pay her uni fees. But her heart had never truly been satisfied with the career path she'd chosen. It had just been her way of showing her family how far she'd come without any help from them. But while working in the shop she'd discovered her creative side and her happy place. So when her life came crashing down hard in her second year of law school she didn't think twice about giving up her degree and working full-time with Lillian. If it weren't for Lillian and her shop, she didn't know where she'd be right now. She had Lillian, Ava, and Jade, to thank for keeping her from falling apart.

She was satisfied with her life now, and she didn't need some *Mr. Pretty* barging into it and upsetting everything. But hopefully she'd never see this *Mr. Pretty* again. Sighing, she turned the lights off and headed for home.

---

## About Sonia Stanizzo

---

Sonia Stanizzo is a contemporary romance writer living in the beautiful south coast of New South Wales, Australia with her husband and three children. When she's not dreaming up stories about couples and their road to finding love, sometimes bumpy but always a lot of fun, she can be found taking pole dancing lessons, reading and writing.

Thank you so much for reading Chasing Trouble. I hope you enjoyed meeting Nick and Ava and loved them as much as I do.

Say Hello


Visit my website to join my reader newsletter for free books, new releases and giveaways. Come and say hello on social media:

www.soniastanizzo.com
soniastanizzo@gmail.com
Facebook.com/soniastanizzowriter
Instagram.com/soniastanizzowriter

More titles by Sonia Stanizzo
Trouble in Love Series
The Trouble with Mr. Pretty
Trouble in Disguise

Acting on Love Series

Risk Taker